The Shadow of Things to Come

THE
SEAGULL
LIBRARY OF
FRENCH
LITERATURE

KOSSI EFOUI

The Shadow of Things to Come

Translated by Chris Turner

LONDON NEW YORK CALCUTTA

This work is published with the support of
Institut français en Inde – Embassy of France in India

The original English edition of this volume was published with the support
of the Centre national du livre (CNL), Ministry of Culture, France

Seagull Books, 2021

ISBN 978 0 85742 873 8

British Library Cataloguing-in-Publication Data
A catalogue record for this book is available from the British Library

Typeset by Seagull Books, Calcutta, India
Printed and bound by WordsWorth India, New Delhi, India

The sole method of suicide that is worthy of respect is to live.

Imre Kertész

FIRSTLY

Shadows have rapidly taken the place of the walls. The ceiling, moth-eaten by darkness, is the lid of a hole. The ground would have disappeared entirely, were it not for the square of moonlight illuminating the rudiments of the decor—the bowl with its hotchpotch of notebooks, their pages ripped out; the bottle, still three-quarters full, of a brown, macerated liquid; the legs of the stool.

General power cut.

However, the days of curfews are long gone—or so they say. And then there's certainly no lack of energy. Not since they discovered the 'commodity' or—since we should call it by its name—oil, whose familiar nickname 'the commodity', when pronounced by the people here, is fraught with a sacred timidity, as though the national naphtha were a god, a private, home-made deity, whose proper name, Oil, no one takes in vain.

Through the window that looks out on to the court-yard, a few cooking fires flaring brightly, ovens with their flames and gas lamps all throwing light on the hustle and bustle of the women in their butterfly clothing, each similarly busied with activity that takes them from the water tap to the raffia mat where a baby sleeps, to the oven or to the tree beneath which a child is taking its bath.

Seen from the outside, it's beyond anyone's imagining that this ordinary scene, repeated from one yard to another as night falls, is my last protection.

'There's no better hiding place than a crowded one,' the hostess had told me, the woman who introduced herself as 'the hostess', when I arrived here on the 13th or 15th of May—I don't remember which. I've been on the alert in this hiding place for perhaps four or five days and time is beginning to warp. Four or five days spent waiting for the single meal that arrives at dusk—the savoury or sweet fritters brought to me by the hostess or the caretaker—or looking at the yard or, more often, at the wall where the books that have been left there are piled up.

What book teaches you what I'm preparing myself to do?

In a short while, when the square of moonlight no longer illuminates me and has left behind the papers scattered round the bowl, it will creep along the pile of books before being snatched away to I know not where. At that point, it will be around three o'clock.

It won't be long then before there's a sound at the door. Four rhythmic knocks and I'll know right away that they have been made by a friendly hand. I'll know that I'm leaving here, my free hand in the hand of the hostess, who'll take me to the exit, to the meeting place she alone knows.

And if things go wrong, the hand that knocks will be the hand of a policeman who'll pretend to support my weak legs, who'll take me to carry out the threat laid down in the document he shoves under my nose, that he reads out to me by the light of a torch before dragging me off.

'Don't wait for them to capture you,' the hostess warned me, pointing to the other window, the one that looks out on to the back of the house, the garden of bougainvillaeas. And not far from the window, the first tree and, beneath the tree, the hole hidden by the tall grass.

The destiny that now draws me far away from here is still called a life, but I have to admit it's like a leap into the void. They say that before he hits the ground a man falling from a great height sees all the moments of his existence come together and drain from him in batches of images.

As for me, it's in batches of mingled words—those words that have borrowed my voice this evening in whispered mode—that the life that brought me here is melting away. And I need to build up a lot of confidence before grabbing my bag and preparing to enter the arena of a battle in which nothing is down to me—neither the choice of weapons, nor the choice of terrain—but in which it is down to me to win.

You mustn't concern yourself too much with who's listening when you want to keep your words intact and unadorned, the way some genuine drunks know how to do, drunks I saw in my father's entourage. The drunks were his only friends, he who never drank yet agreed to contribute to the kitty that was his friends' drinking money for the week—drinking money that included my father's share, though he didn't drink but paid for their company that way, like a child who yields up his possessions to others on condition that they let him pretend 'to be one of the gang'. How otherwise to explain that when he turned up with his hung-over group at the entrance to the Spearhead boarding school—the elite institution to which I'd been admitted at the age of twelve—he who didn't drink walked with that skew-whiff, lopsided gait that he joyfully borrowed from his fellows in perpetual intoxication?

But excuse me, says the speaker, I'm getting ahead of myself. Let's start again.

At my feet, by the legs of the stool I'm sitting on, in the square of the miniature boxing ring carved out by the moonlight, lies a good-sized photo, 8 x 10, in which my father can be seen holding a saxophone case in his hand while I, at about the age of nine, waddle along by his side.

It'll soon be twenty-one years since I was born. As for my childhood, it has to be said that it wasn't without its troubles. But, says the speaker, a childhood that wasn't without its troubles wasn't anything unusual for the children of my generation. On account of the circumstances of an age known as the Time of Annexation, what lay in wait for children at the gates of life were curfews, road-blocks and more roadblocks, houses being plundered, people becoming scarcer, life becoming cheaper and, lastly, family and friends disappearing—thousands of people being banished to a place we should later come to know as The Plantation. That's why those times were also known as the Times of Dispersal.

'On account of the circumstances, prepare yourself to be temporarily removed from your nearest and dear-est/On account of the circumstances, prepare yourself to be temporarily removed from your nearest and dearest/to be temporarily/from your nearest and dearest/removed from your nearest and dearest/prepare yourself.'

This was how they spoke, using few words, those people who carried out the work of dispersal in the Time of Annexation, when they had finished searching a house and—in compliance with some obscure order—emptying it of all the photographs it contained. They opened a trunk, discovered a store of notebooks there and emptied the holdall of its crumpled sheets of paper to root out a tiny photo with all the enthusiasm of an insect hunter who, at the end of a long hunt, has just made some staggering find. One of those tiny photos pasted long ago onto the squared background of the sheet of paper in the centre of a naively drawn, jagged-edged heart, a cobbling-together of words and colours, one of those photos on what was once glazed paper but now looks like frosted glass. And, as they stuffed the images into black bags labelled for that purpose, they never failed to recite the formula clearly, the formula that provided sufficient reason, purely and simply, for their bursting in like that:

'On account of the circumstances, prepare yourself to be temporarily removed from your nearest and dearest'—all said in as forceful a language as you'd use for casting spells. And the person empowered to assault your ear with that language was also empowered to separate bodies. Out of two friends conversing on the pavement, one was taken, the other left behind; out of two lovers stretched out on a bed, one was taken and nothing was left for the other but a formula—'On account of the circumstances, prepare yourself to be temporarily removed from your nearest and dearest'—a formula conjuring away human forms right down to the photographic images wrenched from their frames, which the agents of disappearance tore from the walls and broke on the ground in a mingled crunching of heel and glass, before leaving with one or more occupants for a destination that remained unknown.

We were later to learn, at the end of those times, that it was called The Plantation and that one lived an unwilling life of toil there, until one breathed one's last. That was what awaited those we'd quickly learnt to call here 'the temporarily removed'.

A set expression employed in just that form, the way one borrows an untranslatable foreign phrase, as untranslatable as the words of the international radio when we heard talk of the 'upheavals bitterly afflicting the territory'.

For all those already subject to ritual humiliation, it was as though they were suffering a humiliation even greater.

As though the task of naming this misfortune had been allotted to a distant observer who had come up with this term 'upheavals' (in the plural) as an over-hasty description of something seen indistinctly from a planet beyond the solar system, buried in the depths of space.

And seen from the perspective of this external vantage point, says the speaker, the restrictions, the depredations, the bitterness of the disappearances would have clear similarities with volcanic eruptions or earthquakes, upheavals to be put down to the workings of unseen forces, to those same elementary spirits which, as superstition has it, preside over all disasters—hurricanes, floods and the looting that follows, like those 'upheavals bitterly afflicting the territory' before dispersing in some vague, distant place known as 'the rest of the world'.

And, as for the territory, whoever called it a 'country' and mentioned its name was sure to be cast into nameless torment, struck down by the same law that prohibits blasphemy.

And for many people, nothing you could do without thinking—breathing, eating, drinking, pissing, telling a drunken joke—was accessible without a thousand precautions, a thousand efforts to be seen to conform to regulations, against which one might at any moment be accused of conspiring.

That's how things were in those days, in compliance with arrangements that were constantly being revised, corrected and copiously augmented—arrangements on times for getting up or going to bed, on people's movements, on the sound of certain names, the lists of which were made public, on medicines, milk, salt, sugar, clothing, ways of speaking to one another, even appropriate language. Words themselves seemed to suffer the same restrictions as the circulation of approved commodities. The word 'annexation', for example, was not to be heard anywhere. The way things were in my childhood, we kept silent a lot.

That degradation . . . says the speaker.

That degradation, the seriousness of which can be measured on someone like me, twenty-one today, and the only image that comes back to me when I think about the first years of my childhood, the only thing I see, is a corner and a man disappearing round it, a man in my own image, a man who looks like my father, thirty years old at the time and already a shadow moving off into the distance, framed by two other shadows, the one on the right walking a little way apart, at a good distance from the big case in which he's carrying his saxophone, the shadow on the left sticking tight to him, one hand loosely gripping his elbow—courteously, it would seem—as though he were guiding him in the dark. He's obliging him to walk but without any need actually to force him; in his gesture there is indeed that solicitude with which one steers a groggy companion forward.

The image fades.

The insult remains: a hand. The sensation in my hair is not of a hand that I recognize.

'Your father is going to be temporarily removed.'

Not my father's voice but the voice beside his.

'Your father is going to be temporarily removed.'

The voice came from the shadow enveloping my father on his right.

For a long time, defeated, damaged words poured from my mother's mouth—oddly assorted words in which, as I remember, she called on assistance from a medical operation to transform her into a bird, for it was known there were doctors for changing a man into a woman or a woman into a man.

And that was why she was, for a long time, subjected to extensive examination and taken from one rest home to another. And all I would be told many years later were the mortality figures in which my mother's particular reference number was submerged.

In my memory I was five years old when I was running. A voice kept repeating in the wind and in my ear that it wouldn't be long before they came for my mother, to take her to that sort of institution for the bedridden called a 'rest home', from which there was no way out except to another such institution, where the surgical skill she was requesting to transform her into a creature of the air—to put her out of her misery and leave her human nature behind—was not practised.

The wind lashing my face was a friendly slap forcing me to remember that it wasn't a dream. The wind was buzzing with stories I knew well, stories speaking of children who ended up alone after the removal of their parents, children who were forcibly adopted by distinguished high-society couples in need of new playthings. Or placed in special institutions where, it was said, people taught them to hate their parents—sometimes, it was also said, successfully.

Take little So-and-so, left alone at the age of nine after the removal of his parents and put in a special education centre. After three years he was brought back to the neighbourhood, dressed like some shiny little new god, speaking a sophisticated language in which it eventually became clear that, in his view, what had happened to his parents—their disappearance, their misfortune—was down to their being 'bad elements'. Otherwise, they wouldn't have fallen foul of the regulations.

After much circumlocution for reasons of hospitality, his uncle said, 'But you know they never did anything.' To which he replied, in the best administrative tone, 'Does one ever know?'

His uncle made no further comment, taking fright because he had just realized that, despite appearances, this wasn't his real nephew. He had just realized that the boy standing there before him, laughing, was the simulacrum of his nephew, with a recording of speech inside him which, through physical possession, borrowed the voice and body of his dead, zombified nephew.

In another version of this story, the nephew says, 'The people who disappeared deserved what they got.'

The uncle—'Including your parents?'

The nephew—'Including my parents.'

The uncle—'Why do you say that? You know very well they did nothing.'

'Nothing,' says the nephew, who had begun to laugh. 'Nothing?'

It's the story of the three men together in the prison cell. The first says, 'I got twenty years for telling a joke.' The second says, 'I got fifteen years for laughing.' The third says, 'I got ten years for doing nothing.' 'You're lying,' say the other two, 'doing nothing—that's only a five-year stretch.'

When I say these things today, a flood of stories gushes up from some obscure wellspring of memory, to which the appropriate reaction is sometimes, like the zombie's uncle, to say nothing. How, otherwise, are we to conceive that, through special education, the hatred of innocence can be made acceptable in the eyes of children?

SECONDLY

I was heading for the age of five when my father was 'temporarily removed' and I was nine when the day came that they call—as is taught in schools—The End of the Times of Annexation. It's a date you can read or photograph today, here and there, on a commemorative plaque at the corner of an alleyway or at the base of a monumental statue. The day when everything was suddenly big. The parade in front of the big statue of the great men of Independence and Rebirth was big; the marathon was big, despite the presence of only fifty or so athletes, since the Homeric hearts of the runners with their toned bodies were big, and big the multitudes that needed more than just their hands to salute the selfless gallantry of the people's lean idols—the multitudes equipped with gongs, bowls, pans and a whole array of kitchen utensils in the fists of men, women and children, beating tin against tin, egged on by the radio that had hastily got together a competition among those neighbourhoods most skilled in noise-making.

Next day, around evening, fear paid us another brief visit when the sound of heavy concentrated fire invaded the city, originating from behind the hills, and just for a moment, obeying an old reflex, we took cover.

I was living at the time in a yard populated by some twenty children under the aegis of a benefactress we called Mama Maize, a woman who had taken us in and looked after us for years and who told us, 'No one's immune from miracles,' a talismanic phrase that she repeated as we huddled together, cleaving as close to her as possible, as when, certain evenings, we lay down on the qui vive, the twenty children that there were of us, learning, day after day for years, thanks to the repetition of the talismanic phrase, the art of change that she was teaching us—the art, says the speaker, of ridding oneself of certain needs, the better to stay alive.

That evening, as the firing assaulted our ears, we had the impression we'd been duped by all the festivity, by the glamour of the day—a monstrous mirage, a collective hallucination which this firing was now dissipating.

Neighbours listening to the radio in their shelter had come out, had brought the set outside, had turned up the volume, and we could hear from our yard the cheery voice exhorting the population not to worry about these explosions that were simply fireworks, a word the multilingual announcer translated into the country's other languages as 'shots of joy'.

Mama Maize had jumped up, announcing, 'No one is immune from miracles', and we were already lined up behind her, with Ikko, the biggest of us, bringing up the rear. I walked in front of him, staring at the back of Abi's neck and when I speak of these things today, I can still, says the speaker, see the shape of Abi moving along, see the figure of Abi moving, then fading, stepping firmly down on her left foot and sliding along gently on her right, the foot that had given way towards the end of a roaming that had finally brought her to where Mama Maize found her in a lifeless heap behind the house and took her in. That foot which Mama Maize, with her massages, poultices, ointments and magic formula—'No one is immune from miracles'—had eventually restored to its initial appearance as a foot, with its full five toes, without ever having been able to strengthen it enough to move without trembling. And she seemed, Abi, when she walked, to sway her hips more than is necessary for a girl of her age.

We were in a hurry to get to the place where the fireworks were being set off, to catch up with the crowds of people who weren't giving in to Mama Maize's loud voice and were holding us back as much as they could. We had stopped when we were close enough to feel in our bellies the rumbling of the explosions. The thunderclaps coming from the earth and from our bellies rose halfway up into the sky where they scattered into joyous bursts of light. And we were mingled with the warmth of that firmament, where all the world's butterflies seemed to have arranged to meet and celebrate.

For the first time, we were hearing explosions without panic, and shouts without shudders of fear—shouts of joy, cries of laughter, things never heard before, accompanying the 'shots of joy'. A silt storm rose, a precipitate of colours and fire, a message spelt out in the language of the stars, and even the eyes of Abi, whose lips never smiled, were fired with delight.

As I'm speaking of these things today, says the speaker, I still feel violently overcome by a sensation of a force I'd never experienced before, a force as violent as the one that seized me that day, mind and body, a sensation for which no word had prepared me, and the word 'celebration' wasn't one I knew.

Up until the age of nine the word 'celebration' never conjured up anything for me. I mean no direct experience, not the slightest memory of sensations, images or moods linked to the word. There you have it, says the speaker, that's how you know what a childhood that wasn't without its troubles looks like.

THIRDLY

Among those who'd been 'temporarily removed', a minority had got out alive from the labyrinth of disappearance. The witnesses from that period, to whom they first showed themselves, spoke of seeing people brought back from the dead, living people who'd been given a leg up by dead ones to bring them back to the surface, so much did their bodies resemble the bodies photographed in the mass graves, bodies similarly, severely deformed by the mud, soil and earth with which these resuscitated creatures were still covered, beings of clay who seemed genuinely to have risen up out of the earth, without passing through any mother's belly, without having known, in the belly of a mother, the firing and refining of the clay we are made of.

The only difference between them and the corpses in the graves was that they were moving and could still speak. And, from the little one was able to hear, they said how, after liberating them and taking them to the first town or village that still bore a name given to it by man, the fighters of the Free Forces had wished them luck with biscuits, chewing gum, water and many other precious things.

The rest, says the speaker, you have to imagine. You have to imagine the long path they walked and how tough each stride was that took them from one part of the country to another, through villages scattered about the countryside, where they introduced themselves to those they met, each person repeating his name in case it might mean something to someone, sometimes going so far as to describe their faces as they used to be, to ascribe to themselves the features of long ago, features dictated by their memory in the memories of others. Shapeless faces, formless bodies that went from neighbourhood to neighbourhood and house to house seeking someone among the ruins to tell their story to.

You could see the semblance of a human being arriving, his voice speaking a name—his own or the name of a relative—and someone who wasn't sure they recognized him fell into his arms at the mention of a name. You have to imagine someone falling into those arms until death ensued—absolutely until death ensued, says the speaker. Among the people who fell into those arms, there were some who simply fell flat on the ground and were dead by the time they were picked up again, suffocated by astonishment.

Despite the difficulties, reunions did take place, then, even if the chance of such a thing was wafer-thin, the chance that remained to a child like me—struggling along towards the age of nine—of seeing someone come towards him whom he didn't know or remember, someone who would then be pressed upon him.

'Your father. Get into the photo with your father.'

For the first thing these survivors did when they arrived at last was to have themselves photographed. Some of these photos would soon decorate the walls, the shop doorways or the stations with the following legend: 'Who knows this man?', followed by a telephone number or an address. A new custom at that time but one that hasn't entirely disappeared today.

But I'm sorry, says the speaker. I'm getting ahead of myself. Let's go back a little.

Let's go back over the sense of expectation that followed the first mass return of survivors. Let's go back over the mix of boredom and despair that filled our days—even Ikko's days and he wasn't waiting for anyone, either mother or father, but pretended to be pained by the same waiting as everyone else.

Everyone knew that Ikko's mother had entrusted him at birth to Mama Maize, before disappearing. Like most of the women who became pregnant by enemy soldiers, she had chosen to remove herself voluntarily, before her own family decided to carry out the sentence of ostracism passed on every woman bearing that mark of infamy (and the sentence of death by poisoning that awaited the child).

Children of a thousand—this is what they called those children who preferred to invent a thousand imaginary fathers rather than recognize their true father as a man in enemy uniform and suffer the costs of being made the butt of collective shame.

Ikko settled groundlessly into the same waiting state as us, except that his father—according to his latest account—hadn't disappeared but had gone off to Europe to make his fortune and would be returning shortly.

Time passed. The idea that the last survivor had perhaps already returned, while we were still waiting, was now generally accepted. But it was forbidden to speak of that.

Mama Maize watched over our worry and our weariness. Life hadn't changed. We'd carried on caring for the plants that grew plentifully in the yard and driving away the insects, except for the spiders—increasing in impressive numbers—which we were forbidden to kill because Mama Maize had taught us to use spiders' webs to stop the bleeding from the wounds that didn't eventuate simply from our play. As soon as they had enough energy for boredom, children here, like children everywhere, expended it in fighting.

And since that happened more and more often, Mama Maize more and more often took out the wooden doll, held together with wire and cord—a mutant puppet like us, baby-sized—which she used to teach the bigger children the art of carrying the little ones on their back. 'I'm not asking you to be brothers or sisters, I'm going to teach you to be a mother to everyone.'

Boys or girls, they had to learn how to throw back a shoulder, to lean slightly to one side, to tie the doll to their backs, with its arms out if we were imagining it to be awake or its arms inside the pagne if we were imagining it to be asleep.

And the little ones, who on more than one occasion had seen the doll roll on the ground and stare skywards in disgruntlement, were not afraid to take its place, little ones who had the good grace to roll in the dust with all the valour of a true stunt doll. 'Very good, very good,' said Mama Maize, with the result that the crash landings ended up being such an attractive spectacle that even Abi, who never usually laughed, was surprised to find herself laughing more than the others and taking her turn more often than anyone else.

Once upon a time, as night was falling along the garden paths—along some stretches of land we also called the Walk—Abi had challenged me to carry her on my back through the path between the maize. It has to be said that, in those days, since the cost of clothes was a source of strain, the children often ran round almost naked. Thanks be to the sun, which didn't let us down, otherwise the life we led half-naked would have been wiped out in a night by the slightest cold; but here even the moon is always warm. And it was even warmer the night Abi had found herself on my sweaty back. 'Very good, very good,' she said, in our sweaty affection, Abi's voice simulating the way we heard Mama Maize murmur 'very good, very good' when we went near the hut she withdrew into to make men laugh.

It was at that moment, through my laughter, that I heard Ikko's voice. 'Your father.' Ikko running towards us. 'Your father.' He was right alongside us but his voice was distant. Even when he pressed himself against me, against all apparent logic his voice still sounded far away, and I wondered what evil spell was putting such distance between Ikko's voice and my ear, with Ikko holding tight against my chest and Abi holding tight to my back until we eventually lost our balance and all three fell. Only at that point did the voice come close to my ear, like the sound of a great wave. 'Your father.' And there was a great silence over the whole surface of the earth.

I was running in that corridor of silence which repelled all that wasn't silence towards an inaudible horizon—the wind, the children crying, the voices calling in the distance, the radios crackling out the evening news, children milling round a human apparition, standing there and awaiting something or other, and it was a miracle to me that this man still managed to hold the saxophone case at the end of his arm, his head aslant, barely a skeleton, almost membraneless, wholly incapable of embracing—and voiceless.

The entire choir of the children present in Mama Maize's yard: 'Your father'—that was Ikko; 'Your father'—that was Abi; 'Your father'—the voice of the photographer. With Mama Maize's voice raised above the yelling. 'Your father. You see, no one is immune from miracles. Get into the photograph with your father.' And the sky was full of a tawny sunlight.

And he, my father, uttered not a word, not a sound. He had come back silent, as silent as those severely disfigured children who issue from their mother's bellies with the same stigmata on their bodies as the war-wounded; those children doomed to a hard life, their heads drooping to one side, leaning permanently towards the same shoulder under the weight of some unknown heavy thought; those children who one already knows at their birth will not speak, who will say nothing of what they have seen in the world, having arrived in it wounded before they are big enough to fight.

Here we are then, in the photo. And if there isn't even a hint of joy on my face, only this veil of anxiety, that's not due to the moonlight. It's because my attention was elsewhere. I didn't know what the agents of disappearance had done to my father's voice. My attention was busy pursuing the remembrance of that voice; it was moving like a probe inside my memory around the five-year-old mark.

And nothing in my memory brought back the imprint of his voice, no resonance showing up anywhere in my memory bank of sensations, nothing in the three-year-old vicinity, not the slightest copy of sound images from those years in which he must certainly have laughed at my jumbled-up words or straightened out my rickety sentences. And further back, as a baby, there was nothing, or, even further back, nothing in the belly of my mother, says the speaker.

On my father's left hand, laden as it was with the saxophone case, you see another boy. That's Ikko, who had rushed up at the last minute and pushed his beaming, open face into the photo, his hand raised in a gesture of joy that only he understood.

And later, after bringing us back, Ikko and me, to live with him in that state-funded house to which his condition entitled him, I could never look into my father's eyes without feeling the ferocity of that silence enter me. And I, who very early on acquired the ability to read unspoken thoughts from the tiniest quivering of people's faces, how was I to explain that the only time I was able to see his face without trembling a little, was when he was sleeping. But what can you read from someone's dreams when you yourself, in your own dreams, are so often lost?

I couldn't shake off the sense of watching someone denuded through a hole in some nameless door, and suddenly noticing that it wasn't a stranger I was seeing but a man who looked like me—my father without glory or sparkle, so poorly finished-off, the outline on the ground of a man momentarily left for dead.

How can you be surprised, then, says the speaker, if my face in the photo has the hollowed-out form of a mask turned inside-out?

A few days later, beneath a large marquee with a hundred or so folding desks inside, I see myself, see my father and don't see Ikko, but he wasn't far from the long line of people in which we were waiting our turn to present ourselves to the census enumerators. They were busy collecting what they called 'life and kinship testimony'— the oral testimony of third parties attesting to descendance; notes found in old school exercise books or in diaries, including dates, photographs, all sorts of biographical data, by which the enumerators set great store for establishing files on which the public records system could be rebuilt—embryonic information that would help in the creation of properly authenticated documents that would bear names, forenames, dates and places of birth, names of fathers and mothers. And, where addresses were concerned, the enumerator was accompanied by another figure, who bore the title of administrative officer for communal property, the census also being intended to gauge the housing situation, so that people could be allocated a place in one of the many 'communal housing schemes' the country was currently developing.

The enumerator looked at the photo, the 'evidentiary object' we had brought, whilst I explained to him that I was the one who'd be replying to his questions, since my father didn't speak—didn't speak any more, that is, since his return from The Plantation, and at the mention of that place the enumerator had glanced at the administrative officer. The latter leant his head towards me and I heard him say that my father's condition entitled him to accommodation in a state-funded house, and even to a weekly pension; that this wasn't too much to ask of the goodwill of the community and that he would be pleased, in a moment, to add two other files, a pension file and a housing file, to the one his colleague was still filling in. As the colleague stared again at the photo, then once more at me, I, who had learnt very early to read anyone's thoughts from the tiniest creasing of their face, saw nothing but an infinite series of skull-splitting calculations.

'Your brother, does he speak?'

'My brother?'

Keeping his eyes on me, he pointed with his pen to Ikko. As he did so, Ikko, all smiles, gave me the same look that he had in the photo. I said, 'Yes, my brother, yes he speaks.' And Ikko burst out laughing, before providing his forename. The man simply had to add in my father's surname and that was the happy misunderstanding that made Ikko my administrative brother for life, his presence among us being, I must confess, an element in the calculation of the weekly pension my father would receive. But that's for another time, says the speaker.

We found ourselves, then, living around a communal courtyard with lavatories, a fountain and the trunk of a newly planted flame tree, surrounded by a protective grille. It was a dwelling identical to hundreds of thousands of others, grouped into neighbourhoods classified as 'Ambition I', 'Ambition II', 'Ambition III', and stretching end-to-end for tens of miles, laid out in straight lines, even when they reached into hilly terrain.

We know how these dwellings had sprung up in a mad scramble, in the same genuinely miraculous rush that drove the oil up out of the ground, the nourishing 'commodity', without which these neighbourhoods would not have spread like a blessing over the entire surface of the territory.

FOURTHLY

Around the age of twelve or thirteen, my assiduousness in my studies, my lucky star, my good marks and also that passive couldn't-give-a-damn attitude that's the central thread of my character and which the masters responsible for discipline translated into high marks for good behaviour—all these things and many others that have nothing to do with me, says the speaker, saw me awarded a scholarship to continue my studies as a boarder in a leading institute. And I could now 'evolve', as was predicted in the administrative document that was handed to me personally in a green envelope in the headmaster's office by an official who had come in person from the authorities to wish me 'good luck, good luck, good luck and well done again', while the rain beat against the closed windows.

(And I was free to imagine that that rain had formed in the distant clouds for this day alone and for this precise moment, which it had chosen to acclaim me by rapping on the window.)

The rain rapping out its applause directly against the

broad envelope I'd slipped under my shirt as I left the office, my shirt tucked into my trousers, the run home, the envelope my shirt didn't protect from the rain, the empty place left where the stamp had fallen off—one of those first stamps of Independence, a symbol for which a renowned actress and large-bosomed singer had lent her profile—the stamp I found later, as I was falling asleep, which I pulled from my stomach (to which it had attached itself) and kept for a long time . . . But all that's for another time, says the speaker.

The next day, as I was reading to my father the document the official had handed me in the headmaster's office, the previous day's rain was still stubbornly beating against the windows and excitement, coupled with the dryness of administrative language, made me stumble over more than one ministerial word—'in view of the merits of the case and concluding on the basis of an attentive assessment of the background . . .' As it stood in the document, the aim was for me to 'operate' (the French administrative word is *évoluer*—evolve) 'in the comfortable surroundings of a leading boarding school, the Laboratory Institute'.

The Institute was regarded throughout the territory as a guarantor of one's future, a direct access to the store-house of happiness, a place where even the arrows of outrageous fortune bounced off the armour of knowledge.

That day, I felt like someone who had lived under glass for a long time and who suddenly saw the whole sky open up before him, affording unprecedented vistas.

You have to imagine what the heart of a man might feel if he had been separated from the sea by high walls and had heard the sound of the waves his whole life without ever having seen the ocean; you have to imagine that man's breathing on the morning when the walls crumble away before his eyes.

(But in the following days, I couldn't stop myself thinking that, despite the combined effects of my merits and my background, the institution wouldn't perhaps have opened its doors to me without my father's background—that same background that earned him his legitimate privileges, whereby someone could be required to stand for him in a packed bus, so that he could take the seat reserved for people in his situation.

A thought certainly not best designed for instilling joy. And my joy was brief, notes the speaker.)

Spearhead is the proper name of the Institute I entered at the age of twelve. Each year twenty-five children are selected to study there on grounds of merit and are received in the main quadrangle with highly complimentary speeches, in which they are addressed as 'the advance guard of the Rebirth generation, the generation the hospitals were built for—and the wide hydraulic dams—the people for whom we drilled into the earth, in order to extract the nourishing mother lode—the "commodity"—the people for whom local schools, libraries and neighbourhood cinemas have been opened throughout the territory, together with this flagship establishment, the Spearhead Institute.'

I was among the twenty-five selected that year—children who would be endlessly reminded that the community was giving them the chance to take the last available seat on a shuttle that was sitting on the launch pad. For an eight-year trip. And those who came straight from the distant—and sometimes nomadic—interior of the country would see their families again only four times in all, for a period not exceeding two months.

They didn't have the good fortune of being children of the capital like me; seeing as the Institute was in the capital and an hour's walk from the state-funded house where my father lived with Ikko, I could go home every weekend and my father could take advantage of that proximity to turn up at the entrance to the Institute and even on the main quadrangle, in the company of the amorphous drinkers making up his entourage, he who never drank but enjoyed frequenting drunks.

He reminds me at times of a character in a film, a millionaire who pays people to drink for him the beloved wines his doctor has forbidden him to drink.

My father wasn't a millionaire; moreover, when he'd given his friends their excess of alcohol and had none of his weekly pension left, he needed money.

However, to do what he did, knowing the embarrassment caused in such a place by the presence of his little band, I assumed that it was surely because he was under great pressure from that same band, whom I imagined to be quite desperate, those men whom I imagined surrounding my father and, before dragging him to the gates of the boarding school, subjecting him to serious threats—'Ask your son to chip in. Now that he's got into boarding school he has a bursary. He's a "Spearhead" now that he's got into boarding school. Ask your son to chip in. If not, his ribs might just get broken. Just like that, his ribs, wham! Just like that, the little one's broken, all broken—oh dear.'

I was finding excuses for him that had a horrific underside to them, but they *were* excuses, so that he'd remain beyond reproach in the story that was beginning to spread and which I kept overhearing in the schoolyard, to the effect that there was a child in the school who was being bullied into giving my father money, and that I was that child—I who found every possible excuse for a man who had so little existence that it was impossible to blame him for anything.

FIFTHLY

The Spearhead Institute was an amalgamation of solitudes, in which everyone did everyone else down. We were young people pushed into constant confrontation with one another, from which a number of temporary alliances ensued that we called, for want of a better word, friendships. Fear was the only bond uniting us, the fear of losing face one way or another. Betrayals were accepted as part and parcel of the struggle, and what is known as 'counting on someone' was a sign of weakness.

I began to skip classes to look after Axis Kemal's shop, Antique Editions, while he rode off with a stock of books on a bicycle as refractory as a mule, which he called every name under the sun. Sometimes I met up with him in a schoolyard where he had permission to display his books and cry his wares to the schoolchildren like a fruit seller, to 'get them to taste', as he said when he did readings out loud with a microphone, standing on an amplifier that served as a platform, inviting the children to imitate him by taking over his place on 'the world's smallest stage'.

The children smiled, applauded and waited for the end when they would pounce on the comic books. Then we counted up the pennies that we'd go and pour into the slot of a pinball machine.

I was sixteen when I met Axis Kemal and I realized how friendless I'd been up to that point.

He was the last of the line of an Egyptian family that had settled here and made its fortune over three generations. His grandfather had arrived with three dollars in his sock and, after a number of years, had owned half the sheds on the old port. Not much of that remains, since shipping activities have moved further along the coast, closer to the sources of oil. The Kemal family, suspected of dealings with the enemy during the Annexation days, had lost everything in just one month at the Liberation and left the country.

Axis Kemal's father had listened one by one to the grievances publicly levelled against him on the radio, then to the long list of properties confiscated one after another, a list so long that they hadn't reached the end of it when Kemal senior got up one morning, wrote a letter to a son living in Shanghai, another to his married daughter in London, gave the order to pack his bags, dismissed all the domestic staff and left without knowing what had become of his elder son, Axis Kemal, who had taken to the hills to fight against the Annexation.

Axis Kemal had come back two years after the Liberation—two years in which no one knew he was still alive—and, on his return, he hadn't tried to find out what had happened to the father with whom he had, in fact, only ever exchanged a few hurried words. And it was better that way, he said. As he saw it, something had cooled in a relationship in which he had, for a long time—yet without reason—felt himself obliged to keep up his end, until the day he'd taken the path to the hills.

He ran a bookshop, Antique Editions, whose speciality was not really antiquarian books, as the name might suggest, the sort beloved of lovers of printing and binding and parchments and autographs, but second-, third- and even twelfth-hand ones, which made up the bulk of the stock and justified the shop's name.

He told me he'd 'contracted' the Christian faith in a Judaeo-Protestant form after a serious bicycle accident. He had at that time read the Bible from start to finish, frenetically, and in at least two different versions. Then his trip along the path of God had come to a sudden halt following a revelation that had caused him to lose his faith.

'What?'

'A terrible thing. Imagine this—from the first to the last page, the god of the Bible never laughs. Not once.'

'So what?'

'So, I'm not made in his image.'

I didn't understand. I'd always believed it was normal for a God to be fearsome.

'Imagine that: a creator-God who knows nothing of joy.

All his answers to my questions did was shed a light within me on new, previously unsuspected areas of questioning.

That's what he was for me, the guide for my curiosity. At an age when you learn to believe in 'thinking masters', Axis Kemal was my laughing master and, sheltered beneath that laughter, my mind was kept safe from the diseases of truth, he said—that acne of the soul, he said.

He made me see the world through an obscure science not taught in any school, arguing that man doesn't have five senses but seven perhaps, or maybe eight or nine—who knows? The sense of hearing, the sense of smell, the sense of sight, the sense of touch, the sense of taste, the sense of beauty, the sense of the sacred, the sense of humour—who knows how many?

He spoke in riddles, parables, quotations and snippets of gossip. I spent hours listening to his improbable stories, in which he boasted, for example, of supplying a whole range of forbidden substances to leading lights in the army and police, who enlivened their Sunday picnics with them—that was why he'd never been in any trouble, either on his own account or for his herb plants. But that wasn't all. He didn't only supply substances, but also pretty young men, to gentlemen in high places. And in a country where indulgence is shown to those who chase homosexuals with big sticks so that the law condemning them to five years' imprisonment can be applied, he says he has a solid list bearing the names of members of parliament, magistrates and kingmakers who frequented the beach over by the old port where the boys in high heels, frills and flounces meet up to flirt, boys with girls' names—'girly boys'—with exotic names found for them by Axis Kemal—Edmee, Nisrine, Eurydice, Saphira, Cybele, Mnemosyne.

Thanks to him, I discovered what is known as dubious company, a band of young men, many of whom worked by day as porters, hairdressers, council workers, ambulance drivers and stonemasons, who joined us in the evening at the pinball bar, after changing—by which I'm referring to makeovers that ran to the very tips of their false eyelashes and involved raising themselves up on high heels that would ring out on the dance floor.

When these excessive bodies made their entrance, they were beautiful as only actors know how to be beautiful—beyond the contingent fact of their ordinary bodies. This was the manifestation of a *corpus gloriosum*, their clothes alone revealing and filtering its light.

In their gait, there was the assurance and elegance of those uninterested in conquering their audience or in having others join them. As though the bubble of braggadocio with which they covered themselves to pass through the hostile, ordinary world were an unassailable stronghold or carapace.

From time to time there were police raids and fines were handed out under the law that prohibits the wearing of disguises, masks or hoods and forbids nudity in public places except between the hours of 2 and 6 p.m. at carnival time, not to mention the law that punishes any intercourse between members of the same sex with five years' imprisonment, though the requirement that the perpetrators be caught red-handed was never met, even in the backyard of the bar, where the police would rush in and search right up into the branches of the mango trees.

After they'd gone, the boy who, when he took on his Nubian-princess look, assumed the name of Nisrine, played out the scenes of harassment again, repeated the stinging words—imitating the postures and voices, adding his own comments—and transformed the attack into a spectacle that had both talent and glamour to it. The princess' vitality was affecting, intoxicating. And when she had drunk a little, that vitality took on the air of a wild horse loping through the bar, and something in Nisrine's laugh got through my defences when, with a ringing, high-priestess' voice she announced, 'Only whores and girly boys know how to walk in high heels. Models don't.' Or other comments of the same stamp, such as when she said to me one evening, 'From this evening on, as heaven—and the customers—are my witness, I grant you the exclusive right to call me "my favourite".'

During long stays at Antique Editions, I laid siege to the 'real life' section, the section with the most books in it after the 'graphic novels' section, given how many books were produced with the phrases 'authentic account', 'living history', 'true story', 'personal story', 'eyewitness testimony', and suchlike on them, and how successful they were. And I read everything that had to do with The Plantation, that place from which some, like my father, had returned with the life drained out of them.

I threw myself into those writings, many of which seemed to have been cobbled together hastily, marked as they were by an accumulation of facts, figures and regulations and the repetition of the same images of the big prison village—the groups of huts, the sugarcane fields, the multi-faith religious building, the isolation blocks where people were put on the so-called black diet when the final punishment was meted out (the definitive privation of food and water being a weapon preferable to bullets), and the rats who ate the dead and the clothes of the living.

And the most terrible thing was the impression of déjà vu these accounts began to produce in me, with the same words and expressions repeated from one book to the next and images quickly becoming clichés of an editorial phenomenon dubbed 'the literature of experience'.

However, a concern to look behind the mask, which drove me always to keep a close watch on my father even when he was sleeping—and to follow him—didn't end with his death. It now motivated my choice of reading. This was the last way of spying on him beyond the bounds of death, of grasping something, even now, of that 'experience' he had not spoken about during his lifetime.

When I came across the book entitled *As a Child I Didn't Make Up Stories* by Bala Hella Zamal, I believed initially that Axis Kemal had shelved the book in the wrong place. The tome bore the word 'novel' on the title page. But, says the author, if he chose to call the book a novel, even though it contained only things that actually happened at The Plantation, that's because, for a long time after he came back, he couldn't tell the tiniest fragment of the story without the person he was talking to exclaiming that it was 'unimaginable'.

So 'novel', then, seems the right word for the hope that 'readers will use their imagination'.

This was how I read for the first time—in one of these books—that there were parties thrown for the prisoners by the administration on some official and religious holidays. Parties at which the inmates' own brass band provided the entertainment. And I thought of my father's saxophone.

But could I decently imagine, asks the speaker, that the only motivation—if there was one—for removing my father from home was the urgent need felt by The Plantation's band to acquire the services of a tenor saxophone player? How could I imagine that if they had come for him early one morning, it was for that reason alone? One morning when, of all that breathed in the neighbourhood, the only thing that seemed alive was the wind in the beefwood trees?

After a thorough investigation in all sorts of archive services, I tried to find the tiniest fragment of a sound recording of the pieces played by that band, but nothing remains—an astonishing thing for an administration obsessed with records, noting the most minute details of the life of The Plantation like the quantity of water pumped in the day, the quantity of beatings meted out in the week.

I was no luckier when I tried to meet up with some potential survivor from the band. Perhaps they're all dead? Perhaps none of them wished to answer the personal ads I placed in all the newspapers? Perhaps they all came home like my father with their empty instrument cases—what could an instrument-less musician want to say about a band that no longer exists?

All I gained from that investigation was the discovery that I wasn't alone in researching into these people. A journalist and two documentary-makers on the lookout for an unusual story had contacted me to see if my quest had borne fruit. It had not.

One could easily understand them hiding or remaining silent. Even in The Plantation, writes Bala Hella Zamal, they ranked among the disliked—or even the undesirable. Perhaps because it wasn't only the official celebrations they enlivened with their music but also the private receptions of the high-ranking prison officers, which entitled them to the leftovers containing fish or meat—forgotten flavours for everyone here.

One day, writes Bala Hella Zamal, when one of these musicians had been taken back to the prison huts after a party—one of those special evening parties for which they were lent pressed suits—someone had begun to argue with him. 'Only people like you know what you're bloody doing here. You people, once you've eaten a fish-tail and smelt the smell of other people's festivities, you look like you know what you're bloody doing here. No one knows, apart from the people like you.'

The musician went on with what he was doing—cleaning his instrument. The man attacking him took things up a notch. 'So you don't talk to someone like me? Is that it, eh, mister artist?

A notch higher. 'We're wasting away like this but there's no answer.'

The other man finished cleaning the keys of his instrument, put it away, and said, 'I don't know what I'm doing here, any more than you do. All my actions, like all of yours, are controlled. But there's a single act I alone can decide to perform, the only act that depends on me and me alone. And no one else, not even them . . . ever.'

The other man, shifting up yet another notch: 'And what's that act?'

'Playing the right note.'

The account made no reference to the instrument played by this particular musician but my father's saxophone came to mind. I can't reread these words without feeling again the agitation I felt the first time I read them and heard them resonate within me. The way you hear a song when you read a score, I looked at these words—'playing the right note'—and the voice was suddenly in my ear. Yes, says the speaker, it was my father who lent his voice to these paper words and I was in no doubt whatsoever that he'd said them. I'm not saying he *could* have said them. I suddenly, violently sensed that the musician Bala Hella Zamal speaks of was, in fact, him. That's how it was.

This is the first time I've said these things, says the speaker, because, for a long time, in the words that fell to me, there was no space for describing that particular experience—an experience akin to that of the medium, communication beyond the grave—similar to what the physicist experiences when, seeing the light of a star that has been dead for billions of years, he is still able to make out something of the destiny of the earth from it. And, saying that, I'm thinking, says the speaker, of all those who one day heard certain voices and who went mad from fear of not being able to say so. Or of saying so.

And the voice came to me through those words with the same limpid clarity as the day when, having secretly followed my father, I heard him sing with a bird, a white-crowned robin-chat, which, according to the ornithological books and partworks, is also called a lazy drongo. Books and partworks that I began frantically to give to father as presents from that day onward. Stiff card files, spirally bound, with watercolour illustrations and boxes with the names inside in four languages—the whole collection was the first thing to disappear after his death, stolen and sold off by the inconsolable drunks he frequented, together with the pile of *National Memory Magazines,* to which, like every other person in his position, he was granted a free subscription.

So little existence, says the speaker, even up to that torchlight tattoo that his funeral resembled, paid for from the state's coffers, the wood of the coffin, the hole in the ground, the torches, the flowers in the colours of the flag, the posting-up of his name at the town hall.

With every conceivable spelling mistake.

Even if there's no law against spelling a name the way it sounds, I couldn't but find indefensible the lack of attention that could lead the town hall's scribes to confuse a K and a C, an S and an F on the notice to which every person like my father—and those of his condition—was entitled, credited as he was on that same notice with being a Worthy Member of the Community.

Among the various titles, citations and civil decorations, this title was the best that could be given to the survivors of The Plantation, as was the free subscription to the *National Memory Magazine* and—thanks be to the benevolence of the community—the pension that was paid to him, which wasn't enough to keep the drunkards around him in drink—those hat-wearing, tap-dancing fat soaks who served as his funeral cortege, their hands waving torches in broad daylight, their gaze fixed on the coffin, on the flutterings of the little flag decorating the coffin, a triangle of red and black cotton bearing the inscription in white—THE REGAINING OF THE TERRITORY IS AN ENDLESS IDEAL.

Workers hanging from the pylons stopped work as we passed to take off their safety helmets and place them over their hearts and I didn't know if these elegant salutations were directed towards the national flag blowing in the wind or the remains of my father, a man who had so little existence in his lifetime that he couldn't be credited with anything, except perhaps that he too, like a Titan, had carried the world on his shoulders.

SIXTHLY

In the beginning, when all's said and done, I didn't believe in my father's silence. I've told more than once of how, for years, even in his sleep, I kept an eye on him, watching out for some occasion when he might perhaps allow a few words to form on his lips, deliberately or otherwise.

I remember having said more than once, in a state of great drunkenness, such drunkenness that the quantity of glasses drunk was beyond counting—as was the degree of shame that went with it—a crazed state, in which I told how I spied on my father for years, says the speaker, and how, after that, I dragged around with me the sense of watching someone denuded through a whole in some nameless door. I remember having said these words— 'My father without the glory or sparkle to attract anyone's gaze, the outline on the ground of a man momentarily left for dead.'

I spied on him the way parents watch out for the first intelligible words from their children, anxious they may miss the moment, and I came eventually to believe that my invasive attention contributed to hastening the day and the hour.

Once, secretly, when he went on one of his escapades, abandoning his band of drinkers and disappearing for a whole day, I followed him.

This is the first time I've spoken of how I tailed him to the mass of powdery vegetation that had become of what was once the haunt of the local birds. Trunks of clay imitating trees, branches of salt with a downy coat of limestone upon them—none of it moving when the wind happened to blow against it.

No one went there, apart from the children, who went in search of whole bird skeletons, which they reconstituted on little boards and sold off to people interested in such things.

Those who once knew the crystal waters, the clear phosphorus waters of the river, are frightened today by the sticky metamorphosis that has left them flowing only fitfully, halfway between mud and lava.

The birds that once haunted these waters had fled out to sea, except for a few flocks that came back to sit on the banks for a few hours. It wasn't unusual, after they'd left, to see some of them struggling in the sticky moving mass of that water or dragging themselves off towards the bushes, as though they were heading for the refuge of a nest. But they didn't last long.

They gave the impression of being the animal-world doubles of that cowboy-film character, the card sharp or horse thief, who is tarred and feathered before being driven out of town. And just as the breath quickly went out of such men—not simply because of the dryness of the desert in which they were abandoned without water but because the total closure of the pores of their skin compressed their breathing until they died—the breath quickly went out of the birds too.

I watched my father from my observation post and could see he was looking for something in the bushes. He leant down, peered into crannies and rose with a dead bird in his hand, put it back down again and recommenced his search.

Suddenly I saw him hurrying, then saw him run straight towards a termite's nest and disappear behind it.

There was a cabin there. Through the keyhole I could see my father cleaning a bird, rubbing off all the sticky stuff with a series of brushes made from plants, cleaning feather after feather, pulling out here and there—at the neck or round the belly—a few pieces of fluff which he rolled between his fingers, before throwing what looked like a pellet of black rubber on the ground.

Another time, when I went up to the cabin, I heard birdsong. Not a melodious whistling but a sarabande of vowels bouncing off each other, then another voice replying to it. That was it—wielding vowels in the same way as the bird had done, but—how can I put it?—with a human accent. It was the voice of my father, vocalizing with the bird.

I lowered my eye to the keyhole and here's what I saw—the bird, its feathers stripped of their coating of mud, was not so much flying as hopping, keeping upright by furiously flapping its wings, feathers outstretched in a welter of bright colours, then falling back repeatedly onto my father's shoulder or into his hand.

And that is to say nothing, says the speaker, of the memory I still have of his face, with his cheekbones and chin, his untended goatee beard, luxuriant despite the surrounding leanness and dryness. I looked at his mouth which, up to that point, I'd known only as puckered at the left-hand corner. You have to imagine the lower lip, how it tensed itself and clung to his teeth.

I watched his mouth unknot and yield to a smile of innocence in a face that was all astonishment.

My father was responding to the bird, himself astonished to be chirping away from the larynx, the nostrils, the chest and the throat—I wasn't able to tell from which organs these flights of sound originated, which he picked up and reproduced fluently, following the lines of force laid down by the rises, falls and suspensions of the birdsong, and I don't know which of the two fell silent first. But I saw the bird when its whole body shook with laughter. Yes, says the speaker, with an explosion of sound like laughter, mingled with the beating of wings, as though it were applauding the shared silliness of a good joke.

And I who had learnt to read people's hidden intentions in the creases of their face, could read that my father's was transfigured by invisible constellations, by that unassailable pride you can suddenly see in trance ceremonies in the eyes of people ordinarily regarded as lowly, people generally habituated in daily life to the humility of their condition, habituated to lowering their eyes before everyone and everything that shows airs of grandeur—proletarianized peasants in the cities or servants submissive in their work and sexually compliant— who, in the trance state, gather their faces into fixed images, into gazes that are literally held out to the assembled company as a worthy offering, with that assured noble bearing that no Sun King in all his glory ever transmitted to a painter.

A story dormant in my mind revived itself, as it revives this evening when I speak of these things. It's a story I've already tried to tell once, you'll remember—the bird story that recurred in my mother's ramblings when, after my father had been taken away, her words unravelled and fell apart, and no one understood why she wanted to take leave of humanity through a surgical operation that would transform her into a bird. We remember that this was the cause of her moving from one sanatorium to another. At present, now that the community doctor has been through the archives, all that remains of this story is reduced to a mortality figure—a colossal figure I've had no desire to learn by heart.

While the exchanges between my father's voice and the bird's continued, the one fading into the other, my mind cleaved to the certainty that I was present at a meeting that lay wholly outside the ordinary world, a clandestine rendezvous between my father and mother, who, in accordance with her wishes, had at last been turned into a bird.

I felt nothing of what reality had accustomed me to feel up to that point. I was transported to a land of spirits and parables, but it remained stubbornly tangible, stubbornly concrete, a world whose phenomena I grasped through a sense organ unclear to me, since I could no longer feel my body. I was no longer in the world of understanding. This was the work of a reason that exceeds the bounds of miracle.

Saying this, I'm put in mind of those people spoken of in travellers' tales who rise in the morning and hail the sea with prodigious leaping and shouting, happy that it hasn't disappeared in the night, and who honour the daily return of the sun as a most extraordinary thing.

We have to imagine the face of a priest, last and solitary officiant of this ancient cult, whose only prayers were acts of celebration—whose prayers were neither of supplication, request nor contrition but perpetual celebration. My father, my father's face that morning, was saying something of that kind.

But nothing that might recall the face in the photo. His Friday face, says the speaker, that's what I call that mask.

On Fridays, a day he didn't hang around with his band of brothers, the regulations obliged my father to attend the Discussion Circle. Though he didn't say a word, he was bound to turn up if he didn't want to see the pension indexed to his past sufferings suspended—which it would have been after one month's absence—and if we wanted to retain our entitlement to state-funded housing.

Even for a man who didn't say anything, either before, after or during the hours these meetings lasted, the regulations were inflexible.

And when he came home he had that first day's face on him again, that face carved in the same marble as the regulations, you might say. His Friday face, says the speaker.

And I vowed to talk about this for the umpteenth time with the community doctor who was my official 'mentor'. That title refers to a social figure who made his appearance during my adolescence. He was referred to first as a 'life guide', before the word 'mentor' was chosen, on account of the hint of indoctrination implied in the earlier term. The mentor is an adult with whom you form bonds in adolescence at a collective 'enthronement' ceremony that is supposed to form life-time ties, in the same way as, among certain peoples, boys of the same age are united by blood ties in a ceremony of collective circumcision. You have to imagine the protocol, the flowers, the little thrones, the little flags, the little attentions, the choir, the oaths, the blessings, the embraces, the invitation to the Palace, the pride in all the photos, with heads upraised all round.

No law forced young people to submit themselves to this practice. But the fact that the majority engaged in it proved of such force that it transformed what had at the outset all the features of mere role play into a custom, in which the childless parents and parentless children that we were at the End of the Times of Annexation plugged some of the—substantial—gaps of solitude that had been left in our kinship relations.

I ended up voluntarily associated with the community doctor, whom I'd known since we moved into state-funded housing, since his first visit to my father and since he treated my bouts of insomnia with his infallible prescriptions.

On each of his visits, I reminded him unfailingly of how useless it was for a man in my father's position to obey the regulation that forced him to attend the Discussion Circle every Friday, and, without fail, my mentor acknowledged that I was right. Yes, that must be a punishment for a man of his status and condition, a man who no longer spoke; a double punishment to be forced to listen like that for hours to all those ordeals that he knew so intimately. 'That's pretty poor, that's really pretty poor,' he said. 'But not to despair. We can bring the law to bear.'

'Not to despair,' he repeated, all the time that he was struggling to administer the injections into my father's difficult veins. And, as if to distract my father's attention, he recited a brief digest of rules on elementary hygiene with the workmanlike application of a good student and the clinical voice of a magistrate, re-injecting the same long-term medicines into my father's threadlike veins, writing new prescriptions for my insomnia, assuring my father that, thanks to the providence of the community, people in his situation would never want for community doctors—volunteers like him on motorcycles—to administer the prescribed doses and, where the other things were concerned—'We have to bring the law to bear, I'm sure there are ways to bring the law to bear. Not to despair.'

But I'd no idea what 'ways' he had in mind. And then, bringing the law to bear seemed way beyond my imagining.

He himself can't have believed in it all that much, since he immediately began to express the hope—out loud in front of my father—that perhaps, after all, through being obliged to attend a meeting whose sole aim was to speak, to get people to speak, to let people speak and listen to them speak, the areas of my father's brain in which his capacity for speech had turned in on itself might eventually be activated.

A man who had so little visible existence, except when the community doctor pushed a needle into his forearm. I could see the muscles tense as vigorous as claws beneath his skin.

The community doctor, whom I later chose as official mentor, perhaps because he was the last person still to speak of my mother.

Each time he visited, he swore he wouldn't forget my mother's name in the research he would soon be undertaking, when the archives buried away in the sanatoriums of old were opened.

Thousands of people, many of whom no longer knew their own names, had been rounded up when the sanatoriums closed and dispersed—he said 'dispersed'—into new structures so they could enjoy a period of rest, after which the reconstitution of their identities could be undertaken. And if, by chance, my mother was among the ones recovered—he said 'recovered'—and I remember the silence, a moment when I struggled to read from his thoughts the words he wasn't saying, and he didn't leave me the time to do so, but grasped me by the shoulders with that way of his of squeezing my shoulders to distract my attention from his thoughts, the same way he had of distracting my father's attention from the injections, the same voice he had at that point—'Not to despair'.

We shouldn't despair when we knew that experts had even managed to recover identities from a few bones found in the mass graves—do you hear?—we mustn't despair but be brave.

Yes, he wouldn't forget my mother in his future searches—a fine woman wasn't she?—and I wondered how he could be so sure, and I who had learnt early, for my defence, to read the hidden intentions in the tiniest crease of any face, could see that if the community doctor, while he was talking to me about resurrecting the archives, was falling back on all that beauty of my mother, whom he never knew, then it was certainly because he was in despair.

And he, protesting against my thinking, said, 'There's no doubt about it. Look at yourself. You'll be a handsome chap when you're a grown man.'

The expression still resonates with me now as peculiar—'a grown man', something like the man sitting on this stool today, twenty-one years old, says the speaker, and I've received the blue envelope stamped with these words: Call up for the Frontier Challenge.

'A grown man', that's what my mentor still repeated as he unfolded the blue document stamped with the monumental icon of Mother Rebirth reminding us that 'the reappropriation of the territory is an ideal without end', reminding us that we have ten days to report for the Frontier Challenge. Otherwise you're deemed to have opted voluntarily for 'a hearing before the Behavioural

Council as a deserter in peacetime'. It's true that we're no longer in a time of war.

Over the several nights that followed, I didn't sleep in the same bed twice, moving from one house to another. Sometimes I was wakened during the night and moved to sleep in a different bed, being picked up and taken in by strangers who didn't tell me their names and who asked me, as a mark of gratitude, to forget their faces—strangers whom I asked why they were taking so much trouble and whose only reply was an astonished reaction. Since I met these people, I've stopped asking myself why I made the choice I did. I've seen the impetus of a trust at work that leads one to act without reasons, whether in the strangers who've guided me this far or the people I have an appointment with this evening—those known as crocodile men, whose arrival by sea I'm currently awaiting.

Axis Kemal has described the sailing craft to me in which they confront the so-called Atlantic bar, a primitive coast that runs straight down into the sea, where sea and earth create an abyss of swirling waves that is completely impassable and makes any sort of sailing impossible, except for the natives of the island who possess the acrobatic art of taking to sea in their boats, using their muscles and the speed of their paddles to escape the pull of the vortex.

'According to an old legend,' Axis Kemal had told me, 'when you're searching for a treasure, you have to do so in darkest night, and that treasure is your own life.'

The square of moonlight has shifted towards the wall and has become diamond-shaped as it has passed across the piles of books mingled with heaps of clothes. I can't see the bottle any longer but I know where to put my hand on it. I can still hear my hostess recriminating with me, as she held the plate of fried fritters and steamed fritters in her hands, her eyes on the half-full bottle. 'Drink that up. It will get the bitterness out of you.'

SEVENTHLY

My official mentor was keen to celebrate with me before I left for the Frontier Challenge. There was a contentment in his voice that evening that wasn't linked to the excellent way the rice had been cooked, but to the fact that he, my mentor, sitting on an ill-gotten store of powers patiently acquired in the higher reaches of the university and among the town's leading lights, had managed to obtain a guarantee that I would be assigned to the 'resettlement units'—that is to say, that I would be allocated to distributing provisions and medicines in a unit away from the problem zones. He didn't say combat zones but spoke of psychology and helicopters; he spoke of 'contact and persuasion', and then there was a silence.

And I, who had known from childhood how to decipher thoughts from the tiniest crease of a face, read in his the secret joy he felt at having managed to do for me what he couldn't do for Ikko, namely to pass on the luck within his control, before I left for the Frontier Challenge; the way he had controlled my insomnia since the age of nine thanks to the medical largesse that was his to dispense—that insomnia that gave me nights of vomiting without reason and without sourness, insomnia that had set in again in the last three days, since I'd thrown away the last packets of medicines.

Outside, the bulbs cast a glancing yellow light on the portraits of pensive martyrs hanging from the pylons. But the purity of the flame-yellow light was not enough to dispel that troubling aspect which the presence of the portraits gave to the avenue—men and women, most of whom, as we knew, had been sent to their death by firing squads in the days of the Annexation, whose portraits themselves could find no other location than up against another sort of post.

I knew that what I was preparing to do was far from my mentor's mind—and further still any idea that one of those things would be to forget his name I don't remember what I had to say to hide my secret but my mentor had sensed in the remarks I'd let slip that I wasn't filled with enthusiasm or faith—remarks I no longer actually remember, except that I let slip the word 'war'.

And he brushed aside with suppressed anger what he called 'a slip of no consequence, but honestly, the word "war", honestly . . .' and, with all his might he tried to remain poker-faced, but I who, from childhood, had learnt to read people's hidden intentions in half a crease on a blank face, I could see this 'honestly' making great leaps of vexation from one temple to the other, and for me that was as clear as running a finger along lines of text that I read with my eyes.

'But all the same, the war belongs to the Time of Annexation, and the war is over because the Annexation has come to an end. Didn't the heroes of the Liberation parade in the streets? Haven't the armies of Occupation left, taking the reviled word "war" with them? Isn't it incongruous to speak of war for an operation that bears the name Frontier Challenge, the aim of which is to contain populations that are not rebellious but restive; populations who, through an atavistic, emotional attachment to the forest, are resistant to the advance of mineral prospecting, a source of communal good fortune to which they are visibly opposed? Just as they are opposed to communal honours and the beneficial spin-offs from the "commodity", since they are ready to obstruct the work of modernization that is underway, the penetration of the forest by the modern spirit and the engines of science. But, honestly, isn't it the case that they obstruct these things out of an emotional, atavistic, infantile attachment to the spirits of the forest; isn't it disgraceful to kill our defenceless engineers for an emotive cause? Honestly.'

A year ago, three engineers on a research trip to the region were found dead with their bones picked clean with such meticulousness that it could be attributed only to wild beasts.

Or perhaps to those nomadic populations of the forest zone known as the border people.

We know they had already demoralized the Annexation Forces for a century. Then they had demoralized the census enumerators and the administrative officers for communal property.

Being convinced now that they had hardened their stance, that they were no longer content only to frighten but were going so far as to kill and to pick the bones clean, a programme had been set in place to ensure the containment of these nomadic populations in protected, restricted zones.

And the word 'war', honestly, was an inappropriate one for that programme, the aim of which was, first and foremost, modernization, with railways, schools, hospitals, shops—amenities these populations could quickly take advantage of by trading their craft production based on plant fibre, hevea gum and natural pigments.

The programme termed the Frontier Challenge was supposed to act as an—admittedly strongarm—deterrent force, but we should look beyond the superiority of our weapons, which we would, in fact, use only to shoot into the trees, in order to overawe and flush out the border people, who are reputed to be both cruel and fearful.

Each time a human group was located, siege was laid to them. Since starving them out was a preferable approach to the use of actual bullets, the soldiers would simply shoot into the air to apply pressure, then wait a few days to drive them up to the high ground, where they would be made to accept the weekly distribution of water and provisions that would henceforth beat out the rhythm of their forced, passive sedentarization.

An operation that shouldn't have taken more than a few weeks.

But after a year all that was up on the high ground were a few old men, some children not yet old enough to walk, clinging on to their mothers, and a few ibex. As for able-bodied men, there was no trace of them. Nor was there any trace of some of the young men who had left home to seek adventure.

And so reinforcements were needed to carry out searches. And then some groups that had been successfully stabilized on the high plateaus had simply disappeared into thin air, leaving only emaciated ibex to welcome with a derisive gnashing of teeth what remained of a patrol.

And the able-bodied young men who made up that deterrent force and its successive reinforcements were snatched from their farms, their studies or, in some cases, from a guitar they tried to hang on to the same way as they hung on to the trains—these young people I'd seen when I was fifteen, says the speaker, these young people called upon to advance for a few weeks, they said, barely a few weeks—oh, barely—to advance in serried ranks along invisible lines on the humus-covered forest floor, along the routes of future pipelines that existed as yet only as dotted lines on maps, to track down and identify those known as border people, whom these young people would soon learn to call 'the invisible enemy'.

Those groups ceased their wandering in the forest only to cobble together ephemeral villages out of banana leaves and palm-tree stalks and cook food, before melting away again into the forest vegetation.

Alongside this odd habit of building throwaway housing, which made them difficult to pin down, it should be added that they had lived amidst plants and animals so long that they had learnt the arts of camouflage and poisoning from the former and, from the latter, the ulti-mate defensive stratagem that consists in playing dead.

Several weeks passed, then several months. Then, towards the end of the first year, they gave out the number of the disappeared for the first time—the disappeared, not the dead, since no bodies had been recovered. And despite the presumption that they might still be alive, it was decided that they were the new martyrs who were worthy of a new avenue being built in their name, and then that name had to be found. Since there were already the Martyrs of the Liberation, and they couldn't properly be called the Martyrs of the Rebirth—a title that would imply still-birth—the new thoroughfare was opened as the Avenue of the Martyrs of the Modern Spirit, and their images were printed on pennants, pennants that were waved by people like my mentor—and still are—even though, among the young people we now saw leave, many had the inscrutable faces of glass masks.

And the beaming populace, who are always there to applaud the young people at their departure, continue to shout out that this time it will be all over, after a few months spent tramping round in the great outdoors, a few months completing the containment of the border people.

At the end of a long speech that calmed him down, my mentor judged the silence sufficiently great to let his words of advice ring out. 'My advice is that when you speak, always imagine that someone is translating you into a language you don't know, and you'll pay more attention to what you're saying.'

He spoke now with the same voice as he used to distract my father's attention from the pain of the injections, when he talked of the beneficial effects of medicines and hygiene.

He asked how I was getting on with my medicines, then his voice changed suddenly.

'Have you seen Ikko?'

'Yes.'

And I knew he still greatly regretted not having been able to do for Ikko what he had managed to do for me, to keep him away from the problem zones.

'Still having the bad thoughts?'

'They let him write, but . . .'

'Write? He's writing? I thought he was drawing.'

'He calls that writing.'

'He still calls that writing?'

'He calls that writing.'

'It's good that they let him draw.'

'They let him write but at the end of the week they gather up all the sheets of paper and they go in the incinerator.'

'They have reasons for confiscating his drawings.'

'Reasons of hygiene, they say.'

'Has he complained?'

'Several times.'

'Reasons of hygiene. I don't know if we can bring the law to bear. Perhaps we can bring the law to bear. But it's a good thing at least that they don't stop him drawing. Still having the bad thoughts.'

The bad thoughts—that's the colloquial name given to the disturbance that affects some young people on their return from the Frontier Challenge. Among those who return, there are some who pick up their lives again with an easy mind, who join in with those who, like my mentor, willingly carry pennants at the ceremonies to glorify the martyrs and heroes. And then there are the ones referred to as 'unhinged', for reasons unknown, those who come back speaking a chaotic babble in which the words 'war' and 'images of war' appear, those who ask questions between sentences and who are placed for a time in establishments for the unhinged, establishments that specialize in rehabilitating the weakest, in which medicines and the regular practice of manual, intellectual and creative work helps them, as the specialists believe, to recover the drive to get up in the morning and regain a taste for contributing to the community.

A burst of bad luck, people said. A burst of pain, said the speaker. My father had just died and Ikko had entered a lasting state of affliction and developed such an intense anger that you might have thought that particular death a personal insult to him. His mind was seized by an obsessive quarrelsomeness that led him from one brawl to another, as though he were randomly seeking someone who could grant him redress; he picked fights with so many people and with such belligerence that he was eventually sent to prison for pushing a man off some scaffolding.

I was numbed by the burden of mourning but dazed also by Ikko's distress. A sense of pained astonishment came over me to think that that man who was without speech, without any eloquence of gesture, who had so little existence that you could neither blame him nor give him credit for anything, had succeeded in being enough of a father, in providing sufficient protection as father and mother, that by his mere floating presence, his merely staying alive, he had formed a barrier against all those misadventures Ikko had since allowed himself to drift into. That man who had let him take his name and released him from the mockery that goes with being, as Ikko was, one of the 'children of a thousand'—one of those children who invent a thousand imaginary fathers. In Ikko's mind, the act of the census enumerator had merely countersigned a project ripened by fate. Though he was not his real father, that stranger was, at least, not imaginary.

The administrative chance event that had made the one the son of the other could cause an attachment as strong as that other chance event that threw me, at birth, into the arms of a man of the same flesh and blood.

Since the man Ikko had fought with had survived his fall, my mentor had contrived to use his powers to arrange for him to be offered the opportunity to volunteer for the problem zones and serve his prison sentence that way.

After Ikko left for the Frontier Challenge, I got two letters from him. In the first he told me how much he enjoyed training under water. In the second, which began with news of the season, the wind, the rain and the mud, the sentences broke off suddenly, giving way to illegible signs, a succession of short strokes laid out in tiered rows.

Then, suddenly, at the end of the page, words came back without meaning.

I seem to be looking at the moon
I am looking towards a light
Of which the moon is the shadow

Shortly after his return, the same signs began to be seen all over the city—first covering the walls, then the trees and the pavements, in batches running from one neighbourhood to another—and I was in no doubt Ikko was their author and I worried that one day he would be caught. That wasn't long in coming, after he began to paint them on the pennants and the cheeks of the martyrs hanging on the pylons.

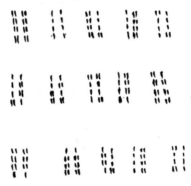

Neither weapons wound nor fire burns the one who has put off the old body.

Being his closest relative in all the world, I found myself attending the Behavioural Council hearing for 'aesthetic sabotage' with him. And when he replied that this was writing, they asked him to read it. He opened his mouth and they very quickly asked him to shut up again. He spoke the word 'combat', as though we were at war; he spoke the word 'enemy'; he spoke the word 'war'. He read these signs and they told how, one evening, during a patrol, they'd seen creatures that were human in appearance loom up and disappear before they'd had time to react in any way. For an hour this had carried on—someone loomed up within their field of vision, as though he'd come out of the earth or a tree trunk, then disappeared immediately, as if transformed into a bush. Then came another and another and another. He'd begun to count them and there was a whole regiment and, as the patrol went on its panic-stricken way, the general impression was that they were being followed, observed, closely shadowed by an invisible enemy. This was perhaps what triggered the enormous volleys of shots in all directions—and not just into the trees—a unilateral burst of fire that went on for a long time, though when at last the firing ceased and they searched the surrounding area, no bodies were found. They found birds, which fell in large numbers, but no bodies possessed of human organs. They went on their way greatly troubled because they now felt even more that they were being followed, observed and closely shadowed by the invisible enemy, but they had squandered what remained of their ammunition.

They asked him to be quiet and he continued to speak or, rather, to read. By a decision of the Council he was sent to one of those establishments that specialize in rehabilitating the weakest. Vagrancy, spreading rumours of war in peacetime and aesthetic sabotage of urban space—these were sufficient to put him into that category.

EIGHTHLY

On Mother's Day, an official mailing was sent to every woman who had lost at least one son in this Frontier Challenge.

Dear Madam,

As you are painfully undergoing a process of mourning that is both yours and that of the entire community, how comforting it is for you to feel with certainty that you belong to a glorious community which takes your plight upon itself. It is from this noble sense of belonging that you draw the strength not to suffer but to endure a challenge that is more than ever your struggle. The reappropriation of the territory is an ideal without end.

The letter was read out on the radio, the sequence being broadcast throughout the day on every news bulletin by the voice of a full-bosomed singer, the same one who served as model for the Mother Rebirth icon, reproductions of which can be seen on the frontages of all buildings and even on school exercise-book covers and postage stamps.

Loudspeakers set up in the streets of the local neighbourhoods carried this message into the yards of the houses, into the little places where mothers still met in small groups, since they couldn't gather in large numbers on the highways any longer, as they did not so long ago when the first bodies came back from the frontier and the women lingered in October Square to weep and remained there for several days with tents, renewing the operation every subsequent Saturday. And it must be said that, when the women here weep publicly for their dead like that, their bodies break free from those hesitations known as modest propriety. They shake about, show their bellies, grab their breasts, throw themselves on the ground and gasp for air. We remember their shouting in October Square, as though they were striving to give flesh once more to all the children who've died since the world began, to bring them back into the world in the wake of their violent deaths. We remember that they tore their underclothes and, by the law that prohibits the wearing of disguises, masks or hoods and forbids nudity on the public highway except at carnival time, these gatherings were ushered out of October Square and broken up.

I'd just had my call-up papers and, shortly afterwards, the guarantee that I wouldn't be exposed to danger. That did nothing to calm my fear, as though the days of curfew had returned undeclared, and that absence of declaration made the fear inexplicable and hence more formidable.

That's what I said that day, trembling, to Axis Kemal.

Axis Kemal watched me cry.

'They aren't always going to put words on things the way padlocks are put on doors.'

He made no gesture, none of those spontaneous gestures I might expect on grounds of sentiment—taking me in his arms or putting his arm round my shoulder— the spontaneous gesture anyone, whatever his culture or religion, would be entitled to expect on grounds of sentiment. And then, in the end, he got up. He turned his back on me for a long while.

'"I often wondered in the past why a man is so seldom capable of living for an ideal. Now I find that many men—almost all—are capable of dying for an ideal, but on condition that it is not one that is personal and freely chosen, but shared by all." Who said that?'

'I don't know.'

'That's excusable. In your state. Hermann Hesse.'

'I don't know.' He turned round. And I, who learnt in my earliest childhood to decipher the depths of anyone's thinking from their face, saw that what I took for a lack of compassion was the therapeutic distance of the physician, who eschews sentiment when it's his knowledge that's in play.

That face which says: 'I have my resources.' I was amazed to see him pull out a bottle of a liquor made by steeping petals and roots, that 'herbal concoction', as he called it, which gets the bitterness out of you and the recipe for which he perfected during the years in which he took to the hills.

'Do you remember the crocodile men?'

He held out the bottle to me with the ecstatic face that usually appeared only when he was plumbing, to some degree, the depths of his inner mysteries.

'According to an old legend, when you're searching for a treasure, you have to do so in total darkness, and that treasure will be your own life. Who said, "The sole method of suicide that is worthy of respect is to live"?'

'I can't remember.'

'Drink it up. It'll get the bitterness out of you. Do you remember the crocodile men?'

Even though the big rocks sticking up out of the territorial waters number half a dozen, only one has been deemed worthy of the name 'island', perhaps because it's the only one that's inhabited. And if those inhabitants are called the crocodile men, that's an expression of the terror felt by those who live elsewhere at human beings who share their living space with the crocodiles in the swamps—according to the only team of explorers they have ever allowed in, for no one could go onto the island unless he was taken there by these men.

And apart from a few famous photographs taken from helicopters, in which you see children disporting themselves in a pool of crocodiles, within reach of their fangs, nothing is known of them or their origins, except that they have for centuries been bound by a pact to the crocodiles with whom they genuinely share their lives. And they've done so without building houses on stilts or developing the art of hunting. No, says the speaker, these human beings, since we must call them that, have married their human smell with the smell of the crocodiles. Otherwise, how can we explain how their children play with the young crocodiles the way others play on the backs of dolphins in theme parks? How can a young human lie down beside a baby crocodile within sight of the mother crocodile if he doesn't smell right?

You have to imagine the incredulity that greets their appearance on the mainland, when they turn up at markets to trade flowers, fruits and bird's feathers for plastic bowls, brassieres and also tee shirts with slogans on them that made them laugh a lot, even though they couldn't read the words: Community/Identity/Stability.

Axis Kemal had already told me that, in the Annexation days, these men travelled as far as the outskirts of The Plantation and helped inmates to escape from under the noses of the guards, who would never have dared face the Atlantic bar in pursuit of them.

And the idea of going to hunt them down on the island using helicopters was quite simply unfeasible, since at some point men would have had to get out of the helicopter and confront the crocodile bodyguard. This was how for years they had thumbed their noses at the administration of The Plantation. There had, of course, been failures, betrayals, arrests and exemplary reprisals. But nothing ever disheartened these men or detracted from the will and cunning with which they'd armed themselves to free other men of whom they knew nothing, except that they were in torment. And in the eyes of the tormentors and their bosses, that act necessarily seemed as senseless as the image of a mother lion adopting a baby antelope.

'You remember the crocodile men?'

It was the first time he'd told me he'd been taken prisoner when he was with the Resistance, then shipped to The Plantation, where he'd spent a year before escaping thanks to these men.

What I didn't know was that, with the help of certain former resistance fighters, he'd managed to make contact again with the crocodile men when the Frontier Challenge was introduced, and to persuade them to set up a network through which the young men who refused the Challenge could escape. I remember asking Axis Kemal why he did that.

'When you come back from war, there's more than one way of freaking out. It was *my* way of freaking out, do you understand?'

'No.'

'So, you're learning something. I really did freak out.'

And over the several nights that followed, five in all, I didn't sleep in the same bed twice, moving from one house to another on the daily instructions of Axis Kemal. Sometimes I was wakened during the night and moved to sleep in a different bed, being picked up and taken in by strangers who didn't tell me their names and who asked me, as a mark of gratitude, to forget their faces.

NINTHLY

One night, at the end of all these somnambulistic wanderings, a man came on a motorcycle to take me to Antique Editions, where Axis Kemal was waiting for me in his reading room—the little corner he'd contrived in the shed with a low table, a stool and his entire collection of dictionaries. He's the only dictionary reader I know. The Dictionary of Symbols, the Synonym Dictionary, the Dictionary of Rare Words, the Dictionary of Proper Names, the Etymological Dictionary, the Dictionary of Psychology, the Dictionary of Superstitions—I'm talking about a man who opens dictionaries without any particular aim in mind, except to lose himself in the jungle of meanings. And this was done to a background of music every day at a set hour, the way others take their walk at a set hour, pray or do their yoga at a set hour. And the only present he ever found to give me was a French dictionary, 'a *Robert* of 650,000 words and their 300,000 meanings, their etymology, date of first use and pronunciation, illustrated with examples and quotations and accompanied by synonyms, antonyms and words of similar meaning.'

Axis Kemal poured me a drink and made me wait while he went to fetch the high-heeled boys, the boys who paint their faces and, when night protects them from the law, give themselves girls' names—rare names like Edmée, Nisrine, Eurydice and Saphira. And the first thing they did was to drag me into the bathroom and shave off my moustache.

Eurydice had covered all the mirrors with towels. Nisrine, leaning against the sink, was smoking a cigarette and studied me closely as the other three stripped off my clothes and made me sit down to take off my shoes. The ash was halfway down the cigarette and Nisrine's gaze was still on me. The others were motionless. The ash fell and the rest of the cigarette fluttered out of the window. Nisrine opened the cupboard and began to point to items of clothing which Saphira, Eurydice and Edmée took and placed against my body. If Nisrine shook his head, they dropped the trousers, blouse or dress on the floor. If he nodded, they folded the item hurriedly and put it on a chair before taking out another.

When the pile was sufficiently well-stocked with samples of varied colours, shapes and cloth, Nisrine hooked a bra stuffed with rags to my chest and sat me down to put a pair of high-heeled shoes on me that left two or three toes peeping out. 'Three inches', she said, 'that's like me only I've got six inches. You feel like you're wearing slippers. It's called foot cleavage. You can see almost all the foot. And now the little strap that empha-sizes the ankle. Get up and walk.'

I could see from the other three's eyes that they were on the alert, anticipating a fall, and I found myself going backwards and forwards to the four corners of the shed while Axis Kemal's head remained stuck in a dictionary.

'I had to put my hands on my hips', says the speaker. 'The support polygon', says Nisrine, 'the poise you have when you walk is down to the support polygon. When you swing that polygon, you shift the fulcrum from one buttock to the other; that's what gives you your poise, and it's essential to bend your knees slightly, since you're pulling on the toes, the four of them. You stand on three toes, but you pull on four, understand? The fifth doesn't count. There you are, there you are! The only women who really know how to walk in high heels are prostitutes and tango dancers . . . think on that . . . not models. Don't walk like a model.'

And when the time came to varnish my finger- and toenails in mauve, we went back into the bathroom, into the gossamer ambience of material, perfumes and laughter, contemplating one another, viewing one another as multiple similar reflections. Eurydice hadn't yet taken down the towels that she'd put over the mirrors and we had only our eyes to reflect one another.

Then they began to sing in English 'The Low Spark of High-Heeled Boys' and we began to shake about against one another, as though we were only there to party to this song, 'The Low Spark of High-Heeled Boys', which was about boys like us who hadn't to make a noise with their high heels when they came home in the early morning, because of the complications, as Nisrine said. 'Where did you learn English?' asked Edmée. 'On the frontier?' And as we were shaking with our laughter, I was sorry, I who learnt very early on to read the depths of other people's hidden intentions from their faces, sorry at that precise moment that there were no mirrors or even a tiny pool of water in the sink in which to read the thoughts I was hiding from myself. And my belly was filled with great bitterness.

Axis Kemal was standing in the bathroom doorway.

'Your train leaves in an hour.'

Then everything went very quickly, driven by Nisrine's nervousness as he put a veil over my head that made my ears, forehead and eyebrows disappear, and my hands were all damp as I checked the contents of my father's saxophone case I was using as a suitcase, or rather checked that there were no masculine items in it that might betray me. And I remember the fear in Axis Kemal's voice as he repeated his advice, and that attention too in the boys' eyes—their features recomposed as when tears are checked back.

Nisrine said, 'I think I'm going to scream', and the others squeezed up against her.

The high heels frightened me. I felt as though I was performing the act of walking without going anywhere. I was in a dream in which you can see the light of a door and are running towards it, but eventually realize, after a tiring spell, that you haven't covered an inch of the distance that lies between you and it, though you haven't stopped running for a moment. A dream consisting entirely of an arrested image, in which you have the impression that nothing's happening except that there's an open door where a light continues to shine infinitely. Apart, of course, from your genuine tiredness when you wake.

I thought of Mama Maize. I went to see her when I got my call-up papers to give her the address where she could visit Ikko.

The last time I saw her was four years after I left her yard with Ikko and my father, because she was one of the women who'd had to take flight in the weeks following the fireworks celebrations that marked the Liberation.

The end of the Annexation time involved that too—another style of celebration. Golgotha-like scenes in the public square where someone was dragged out, fixed not to a cross or a mast but to the cable of a crane that served the same purpose—for hanging up a live creature of flesh and bone, a creature stripped of its clothing, to be whipped, to be lacerated mercilessly in an ordeal forty times worse than the punishment of flogging, beaten as never a drum was beaten before, as though there were no skin. And those in the neighbourhoods who chose their fellows to administer these strokes, those who put themselves forward to deliver them and all who opened their mouths wide to count them said that, if these persons were being strung up and beaten—a large number of them women—then it was for what they called 'inappropriate frequentations' during the time of Annexation.

Rumours abounded on the use Mama Maize made of her body with men in exchange for a maize pancake and, among the men who came to visit her, it wasn't difficult to find some who were 'inappropriate frequentations'. I speak of these things today, says the speaker, so as not to forget that the maize pancake was the means of subsistence.

Mama Maize had taken fright and left town, hiding for four years in a place whose name she will not mention even to this day—a place where they didn't know what she did in life, either for good or ill. Four years, says the speaker, even though this collective human behaviour that had so scared her had lasted no more than a fortnight, before being declared shameful and described as 'excesses'. As though those people were out of control when they committed those acts. And the day the acts ended—declared shameful in high places—became a red-letter day in the annals of history, to be known as the Day of Rectification.

Some older heads said that this providential sense of shame that brought the daily practice of public punishment to an end came just at the point when the names of Mrs So-and-so or Mrs Such-and-such were beginning to appear on the lists drawn up for the lashings. And Mr So-and-so or Mr Such-and-such were heroes, some of whom had given an arm for the motherland, or an eye or a son. It was no surprise, then, that when these same glorious names, borne by wives, began to appear on the lists of infamy, all this came to an end and the Day of Rectification was decreed from on high.

And the ladies who bore these worthy names left for long holidays, and the women who'd disappeared into the bush returned amid the silence and indifference that was henceforth to surround this wordless business, with no one being in any hurry to invent the appropriate words for it. Too few words—apart from 'inappropriate frequentations', 'excesses' and 'Day of Rectification'—too few words to apply to it now or ever. With the result that I was, for a long time, unable to talk about this story with anyone—not even my mentor, who would have said, 'Yes, I acknowledge that it's poor, it's really poor, these excesses', nor with Mama Maize who'd waited four years after things died down to overcome her fear and return to the yard. I was able to see her only once, since my mentor had gone and threatened that he'd set the law on her, in view of her status as a prostitute, if she kept on receiving visits from a boy of fourteen.

That's how, under the protection of my mentor, we lost touch with one another in the same neighbourhood.

I gave Mama Maize the bit of paper Ikko had slipped me the last time I'd been to see him. The paper they generously agreed to provide him with to preserve the walls of the institution from his calligraphic assaults. The last writings, which he was preparing to pin to his bedroom door for the fourth time, and which he ended up slipping into my pocket:

This hut is not of this world. But I am delighted to share the neighbourhood.

TENTHLY

In the train, sleep wouldn't come to me. My mind was preoccupied with the cast of Nisrine's face when she'd said, 'I think I'm going to scream', like someone who says 'I think I'm going to vomit', but doesn't. A face with its features woven like a curtain, on which I could read nothing except perhaps that voiceless scream, something recalling certain forms of hole made in the trunk of a tree and reawakening a memory of a similar face glimpsed in a film I've been mulling over for an hour. You have to imagine a man who up to that point had, as they say, every reason to be happy—a home and a partner; children and the promise of being a father again, since his wife was pregnant; a job which, without making him rich, put him and his family beyond the reach of need; the good fortune to live in a time of peace, at least so far as his country, Sweden—if I remember rightly—was concerned; and faith in a God standing watch over all these things. And then one day he reads in a newspaper that in China children are brought up to hate.

It isn't known precisely what words the man had read in the paper; it's a scene reported by his wife. But, whatever the content of the article, he was affected, despite the distance from China—profoundly affected—by the presence in the world of an evil he'd never previously imagined—the teaching of hatred to children.

Whether true or not, he dies of it and here's how.

He becomes greatly afflicted in his mind and gradually collapses into himself. His wife presses him to consult the man of God and he does so.

And when we see him leaving that man, we already know he won't be going home.

The man of God spoke to him about God's silence. Above all, he told him, you can live with that silence. You have to live with it; you have to live with God's silence the way he himself had lived with that silence since the death of his wife. Some hours later the man is found drowned. And the issue for the man of God is not to find the words to speak to the widow about God's silence, but to announce to the pregnant woman that they had just fished out the body of her husband who, upon leaving the church, had thrown himself into the canal.

I can see again the man leaving the church. I see him moving resolutely, deliberately towards his death and I've asked myself whether, in all the philosophies Axis Kemal made me read, there was a single sentence I could have spoken to that man, a quotation I could have offered him, a sudden flash of inspiration from my extensive reading that could have halted the funereal march on which he felt doomed to engage. I've thought about this and found nothing. And then I despaired of the silence of the philosophers, the way the man in the film despaired of the silence of God.

Sleep came to claim me, but not often, just at intervals; then as soon as I forgot myself, it left me again and waking was like a newly begun falling.

My mind drifted for quite some time; then my body was suddenly shot upright by a succession of jolts. I don't remember the name of the town where the train stopped. I barely had the time to catch a few consonants on a signboard—TR-GW-TR.

Each time I woke up, the scene in the film where the man comes out of the church came back to mind; I saw the look on his face, the distortion similar to that on Nisrine's face.

I remember a moment, I don't know when it was or at what city stop the two girls in air hostess uniforms got on. I remember they'd complimented me on my high heels and my clothes but I don't actually remember seeing them board the train, so I must have been sleeping when their compliments woke me, and since it's unthinkable to wake someone up just to compliment them, I have to conclude that I may have dreamt the whole scene. I'm thinking, for example, of their laughter as they listened to the announcements by the guard, whose voice 'lacked professionalism' since, in their view, it tended to generate anxiety, and they'd set about correcting him after the fashion of schoolteachers, going over the guard's words disdainfully, with the correct tone of voice, they who knew how to make those same announcements impeccably at a higher altitude and in foreign languages—'ladies and gentlemen'.

'We're very demanding, very demanding. That's how it is.'

They got off at the next stop. I was beginning to feel glad to be alone in the compartment when I saw a young, barefooted man rush in and take the seat opposite mine. He was all smiles and hello and how's life and what town are you going to? I suddenly felt panicky. My leg was numb but the idea of crossing and uncrossing my legs was even more paralysing.

A glance at his bare feet and his coloured scarves told me that the young man was a member of the Nameless Brotherhood, the group whose followers say they have no need of a name since they are recognized by their appearance. People call them the barefoot dancers because of their marked loathing of shoes and their habit of gathering together at roadsides, stations or in marketplaces to dance to the point of exhaustion. It's an exhaustion they're not averse to encouraging with great glassfuls of a rotgut that drives them to scenes of spectacular drunkenness—to the point where they actually strip off their clothes. They are also called 'the wild with joy'.

From the point of view of the community, in which there could be no such thing as a dropout, they were not rejected but regarded, rather, as 'loose members'. And the only law the community had managed to level against them was an old one from the days of Annexation that prohibited the wearing of disguises, masks or hoods, and nudity in public places except at carnival time between the hours of 2 and 6 p.m. That was not enough to contain the ardent expression of their freedom of worship.

He launched into a homily which, fortunately, required no other vocal participation from me than a little humming to show I was paying attention.

The essence of the doctrine is a total loathing of work, renunciation of the 'commodity' and its by-products, which are, in their view, merely a disaster disguised as a blessing, leaving human beings to perish where they stand, alongside waters they can no longer drink. And then it goes something like this—

'Among us, we celebrate when someone dies. We say he has been liberated from the pollution of suffering. Among us, when a man is drunk, we call him free. Among us, it isn't a question of living as though you were going to die tomorrow but of living as though you were already dead. Then everything becomes possible.'

Hence the vistas of suicide on to which this philosophy joyously opened. He laid before me the conditions, the protocol, the recipe for the suicidal act and I noted mentally that the twelve stages leading to deliverance were so long and complicated that there was more than ample time and opportunity to change one's mind. But he assured me that, in exceptional cases, some people did manage it.

When he began to talk about sacred eroticism, my sense of panic returned. I took from my bag the book I'd brought with me for the trip, the last of the books I'd been taking everywhere with me for a year—from my bedside to political demonstrations, taking in every bar in the city on the way.

I took advantage of a moment of silence to open the book at random and heard him reading out loud the words on the cover—'*As a Child, I Never Made Up Stories. A Novel*.'* I seriously pretended to be immersed in it and it worked. I was relieved to hear him hum a song and fall asleep amid his scarves.

The green of the tall grasses and the creamy white of the clouds mingled in my vision in this morning light, the green of the tall grasses reaching to the horizon. It was like a stretch of water with wavelets rippling across it in continuous motion and the impression was that all this green could suddenly rise into the air, snatching up packs of red ants with it from giant anthills visible from time to time.

There were clusters of cones too, imitating the anthills, except for the smooth regularity of their assembly:

---

* 'As a Child, I Never Made Up Stories' is also the translated title of *Enfant, je n'inventais pas d'histoires*, a play by Kossi Efoui that was staged in 2009 by the Compagnie Théâtre inutile and directed by Nicolas Saelens.

dwellings in the old style, emptied of the humanity that had once enlivened them with fire, laughter, shouting and songs of joy or lamentation—lives rendered footloose, caught up in the rush for wealth which drove them now from 'new towns' to towns merely projected, from mine to mine and port to port, wherever activities around the 'commodity' were being converted into an accumulation of buildings and factories.

A flow of lives being endlessly sucked up, lives rendered footloose, lives hurried from one factory to another, yet losing, as they passed from port to port, a little of their capacity to hurry, and left, in the end, with only the capacity to drift.

'You've only to follow the crowd,' Axis Kemal told me, a great mass of humanity expelled by the resonant yawning of the doors opening in the sides of the trains—three or four of them that came into the station together.

We had indeed arrived at the memorial city, the former site of The Plantation, the city that has retained the memory of that name, even though the sugar cane economy no longer presents any great interest since the coming of the 'commodity', and even though the actual plantations, where five hundred thousand men and women had for years been exhausted by toil and the lash, were now under threat of reverting to forest three miles from here, as we would later learn from the mouths of the guides.

I attached myself to the crowd and moved with it down streets that seemed to shrink by the minute, streets stifled by such quantities of humanity to the square inch.

After an hour we suddenly speeded up, then had a sense not of moving, but of being sucked in a particular direction, at the same time as being pushed from behind.

It happened so quickly that I can't say how I found myself on that boundless square, capable of containing three times as many people as were there, and the multitude present already ran into very sizeable figures.

What remains of The Plantation's story is a two-dimensional scene—the ground flat and floored with black, polished stones standing shoulder to shoulder, the waiting guides holding up signs marked A, B, C, D and so on, and markers on the ground laid out like pathways. Nothing remains of the groups of huts, the places of solitary confinement or the multi-faith religious building. Those things had all been swept from the earth and the map by the will of the occupiers at the point when they had been routed.

I was among the eager crowd of pilgrims—that is the name given to the visitors to the national memorial—moving towards signboard A, as instructed by Axis Kemal. I was jostled by bunches of cheerful schoolchildren, themselves spurred on by the conscientious enthusiasm of the teachers who had taken them on these paths of pilgrimage in order to expose them to the scene and narrative of suffering that adults are convinced they will see disappear from the earth if only they can hammer them into the heads of children.

A memory came to my mind and lingered—the headmaster of the Spearhead Institute where I was a student, his pride when he came to announce to us the name of the martyr our class was invited to 'adopt' for the year and his gusto during the ceremony that ended in the students going back with the portrait of the martyr to be hung up in their bedrooms, along with the biographical booklet containing a photograph of him as a child or a baby. It was, the headmaster explained to us, as though we were keeping alive the memory of a courageous little brother, sister or classmate.

In days gone by, on this great square stood the prison-village, said the lady at signboard A. This was the reception point for the new arrivals, which was where the procedure began by which the troublemakers were sifted out, or those who were thought to be troublemakers —some of whom had simply resisted a little at the time of their arrest—all those who'd earned themselves the 'reception diet', that's to say, those who'd be fed on water alone for the number of days needed to put together the team responsible for questioning them. I noticed in passing that she'd made no mention of the brass band that played at the entrance to the prison-village. She was already taking us off towards the huts or, rather, towards the places where they'd been built before the occupying forces had burnt them down during their final collapse.

There was nothing to be seen any more and the guides had nothing to show, which meant that you had to be a good storyteller—even a 'smooth talker'—to be a guide at this complete ruin or, alternatively, be skilled in gesture and mime to conjure up buildings, dimensions, distances, proportions, streets and railways for the pilgrims in these utterly empty surroundings. Only the power station three miles away, which was of no interest to the pilgrims, had been spared and it still fuels the new town which consists of social housing built on piles, because of the flooding that is common in this region, explained the guide.

But if you managed to insulate yourself from this rush of words, as I am able to do, you could read from her face the words that couldn't pass her lips, but were evident from her copious gesturing—'Ladies and Gentlemen, there is total emptiness here.'

Total emptiness, except for the crowd spreading out behind their agitated guides, who from time to time slowed or halted the group in their zealous progress to direct the collective attention to a virtual point here, another one there or some imaginary corner somewhere. And the pilgrims resorted to their own mental screens to give concrete form to descriptions that had a ten times greater effect on the imagination for the absence of physical evidence.

We then had to walk a good half mile to another open space whose decor consisted in some random stretches of wall and a few doors lined up like samples, still covered in their original graffiti—bits of flotsam and jetsam spared by the end of history, left over from demolition and fires. You have to queue for an hour or even two if you want to get close enough to read the biggest of the graffiti—'If someone kills your mother, don't kill him, send him here.'

Another thirty minutes of close marching took us to the main avenue with the same thoughtful martyrs hanging on the pylons and the signs proclaiming—'We welcome you here as pilgrims, not as tourists,' even if the shops here do look like any old tourist shop in any old tourist town and the local specialities relate as much to the region as to historical memory.

The end of the visit took us to a neighbourhood I didn't know existed. It was a sad and fascinating discovery—in that area the majority of the population actually consists of survivors from The Plantation, who had requested of their own free will to return and settle here when the new town was built.

The group of pilgrims was beginning to disperse towards the shops and I didn't know what to do since the guide was watching. Axis Kemal had promised that someone would be waiting for me. And here I was trying to contain my troubled thoughts so that they couldn't be read off from my face.

'Can I help you?'

'I don't know,' I replied, following Axis Kemal's instructions.

She beckoned me discreetly and I followed. We found ourselves in an alley crammed with people playing cards outside shops, with water sellers, singers and exaggeratedly overdressed girls in precipitously high heels. A group of barefoot dancers were springing about noisily on the street corner and the lady took advantage of the racket they were making to raise her voice.

'Who sent you?'

'I don't know.'

'There's no better hiding place than a crowded one.'

She didn't want to know my name. She didn't say her name. She said, 'I am the hostess.'

She put me in this room. A wooden bed. This stool on which I'm sitting. The books piled up at random. The window out on to the yard, the one where the moonlight comes in, the one I can open only when the grille is closed for the night. The window facing the garden, the one I mustn't open or 'only if necessary and I hope you won't need to', she added, without explaining anything about that need or her hope. She simply pointed out that the garden has bougainvillaeas in it and, beneath the first of them, which isn't far from the window, there's a hole concealed by tall grasses. I know I mustn't ask questions, that silence is my way of maintaining vigilance.

She didn't tell me the name of the young man who joined us later with a bottle he placed on the ground before leaving without a word.

'The caretaker', she said.

She took the bottle, opened it, drank directly from it and put it back on the pile of books that completes the furnishings.

'Drink that up. It will get the bitterness out of you.'

ELEVENTHLY

What book teaches what I'm preparing myself to do—to strike out on a road where walking is not taking one step after another but making one jump after another? What book provides knowledge of the sensations this demands of the body, sensations which can be learnt only from certain animals—tortoises, passenger pigeons, trout, salmon?

What books? The books of the philosophers Axis Kemal's enlightened thinking had opened up to me? An enlightenment he began to impart to me quite early on, around the age of sixteen, when he told me about Plato and the myth of the cave. I ended up believing I was making some progress on the path towards a sort of knowledge, though of precisely what nature I cannot say today, any more than I can say whether I was learning to die like Socrates or to live like Diogenes or, simply, to manage to build up a sort of personal wisdom for myself, to have a philosophy in life, as they say, to have a life at least, says the speaker, something I can at least call a life—twenty-one years old and so many books read, so many films seen, so many stories heard, so many quotations—my whole collection of knowledge since the age of twelve.

I still sometimes open the only book I brought with me and, so as not to let the time pass sleeplessly by, I learn a few passages by heart, before abandoning it here the way all the others have been abandoned.

I close my eyes to sleep and don't always manage to. My thoughts grow blurred and I can't read. On my inner mental screen I re-project films that I've seen, from which images come back to me, distorted by tiredness and sleeplessness, in the mixed mode of dreams, images that I organize out loud to recover the thread of the story, the way one talks in one's sleep.

Because of the circumstances, I don't know whose silhouette I'll make out shortly in the empty yard. If it's that of the hostess, her hand will touch the door just enough for me to hear her fingers scratching the wood, and then I'll know I'll be leaving here with my free hand, the one that isn't holding the saxophone case, in the hand of someone who knows the way out. 'If it isn't me, don't wait for them to capture you,' the hostess told me. She explained how—the window facing the garden, the one that opens on to the bougainvillaeas and the shelter of the hole hidden by tall grasses.

I shan't wait for it to be some other hand than hers, a hand that's used to hammering on doors, accompanied by the voice of someone who won't fear to bark so loudly that I'll have no need to hear his words to understand—

'desertion in peacetime'—the hand of an officer who'll pretend to be supporting my weak legs to take me away and fulfil the threat prescribed in the document he'll push under my nose and recite to me by torchlight, before hauling me before the Behavioural Council, a body of specialists authorized to probe you from head to heart and heart to head and come to the inevitable, unanimous finding of an 'egotistical deviation', 'a gradual loss of reason for living communally'.

I went with Ikko to his first hearing by five specialists when he came back unhinged by the Frontier Challenge and I know what it is to sit opposite those especially select characters.

Though merely there to accompany him, I had the unpleasant sensation of being potentially guilty. What a terrible thing it would be to be genuinely guilty in their eyes—guilty before the tribunal of the thoughts flashing across their eyes like a hurricane?

And then there's this ritual of welcome which, as soon as you get in, consists in them ostentatiously turning round those little cards on the table with their names marked on them: expert in this, expert in that—all of them doctors.

Why did they put them out to begin with if they were going to turn them round again suddenly, feigning surprise at your entry. 'Hello, who told you to come in?'— and they turned round the little cards with their names marked on them—and I replied that we heard the bell go in the waiting room—'Oh, did you?'—and that the number that flashed up matched the number written on the paper I was searching for in my pockets—'Oh did it?'—'Yes, I'm the closest relative, the last living relative'—while I was searching for the bit of paper—'In that case, take a seat!'—and they kept on turning the cards round on which their names were marked, to give us a clear sense they were afraid we might remember their names in future, seeing how dangerous we were.

All these feigned precautions to prevent you from remembering their names, people as well-protected as they were—'Hello, who told you to come in?'

You begin to understand that it's not about your attitude but your position. And the conclusions in nine cases out of ten are always the same—'egotistical deviation', 'gradual loss of reason for living communally' and the consequences are always the same— sufficiently long and sufficiently frequent stays in one of those establishments devoted to rehabilitating the weakest, in which medicines and the regular performance of manual, intellectual and creative work help people, as the specialists believe, to regain the drive to get up in the morning with a desire to play their part. And that belief is proclaimed in green letters in the reception of the Centre for Civic and Spiritual Education: WORK HEALS.

TWELFTHLY

It's a long time now since the legs of the stool were lit by a square of moonlight. It has shifted towards the wall, crept along the pile of books and stretched itself out into a diamond shape. It will eventually collapse back on itself, becoming just a thin line, and I know there's less than an hour now before someone knocks on the door.

In the city at this very moment, other young men, each isolated in a room similar to this, are waiting like me—around twenty of them, the hostess told me, each removing any bulky items from his bag, with the same doubts that breed fear, each removing a little of the bitterness with every gulp of the sturdy mixture. The work of forgetting has to be completed, before striking out on a road where walking is not taking one step after another, but making one jump after another, in a flight that is a leap into the void—some twenty others dreaming like me of those crocodile men who, at this very moment, are braving the dangers of the sea for us.

I think of those who've passed this way before me, who've waited like me for the same signal, emptying their bags of things—things that in some cases had previously been of value to them: a book or some other fetish object that has suddenly acquired monumental dimensions—to create space for food, for the large amount of food needed on the crossing; emptying their bags as I do this evening, hesitating between a shirt and a pair of trousers and eventually leaving both behind, so that, with time and the number of people who have passed through, the books have piled up here, jammed down one on the other to form a piece of furniture on which to stand a bottle— 'Drink that up. It'll get the bitterness out of you.'

I think of those young men who have, like me, sworn not to remember any names, including the one that has, up to this point, been their own.

Those who knew one another before will feign lack of recognition if, by chance, they meet on the boat. Once at our destination we'll find new names by which to know one another. And, from that point on, all the life we've had up to then will be regarded as a previous life. And, as such, it will be consigned to oblivion. And whoever tells of that life will be called a liar.

You have to break the habit of being yourself, before carrying on your journey, lose the habit of giving your name or referring to your birth. Your date and place of birth, the glorious name of your country of origin, your precious lineage—all these signs we've been brought up to treat as our shop-window, all these external markers we use to imagine ourselves as ourselves, these possessives which I agree to consign to the bonfire of forgetting.

I've struck a few matches in the little basin and the smoke is already rising from the jumble of papers. The notebooks with the pages ripped out, the photo with the three of us in it—my father, Ikko and me—the two letters from Ikko, the false identity papers in which I'm called Ionia Zamal.

A scene out of a film, a scene from war archives, presses itself on my memory—three Buddhist monks, sitting in the lotus position and sacrificing themselves by fire in a Saigon street. War was at the gates of the city and this was their last act of protest. I can see them again in flames. I think once more of their silence and the stillness of their bodies as the flames grew; the three men burning alive remained motionless. As though they were already dead bodies before the fire even began, bodies politely awaiting the end of the formalities of living, already withdrawn into a masterful, confident part of themselves that would win out over pain and fear.

Some words come back to me, written by Ikko and mixed in among the vertical, hanging strokes that covered the rectangle of paper he handed me on my last visit. *This dwelling is not of this world. But I am delighted to share the neighbourhood.*

I don't have the knowledge the three monks have, nor their assurance which is otherworldly, an assurance one finds perhaps only in the animal world, when the trapped beast is capable of gnawing away its paw to free itself.

I don't have the fox's strength of mind, but here I am preparing myself to step into the arena of a battle in which I would like to have possessed that quality of confidence, the same quality of confidence it takes to let yourself be killed.

And saying that, I'm thinking, says the speaker, of those men I was taught to venerate as instructors of humanity and who have only one thing in common— that quality of confidence required to let yourself be killed. Socrates? A man who let himself be killed. Giordano Bruno? A man who let himself be killed. Gandhi? A man who let himself be killed. And what are we to say of the fascination of the Golgotha myth? What are we to say of the effectiveness of Christian propaganda, fashioned out of the figure of a man who in actual fact performed no other miracle on earth than to let himself be killed?

You will let yourself be killed—this is the single instruction that raises you above all morality, all power, all commandments, all domination and, in the face of which no god can do anything but keep his mouth shut.

The caretaker's radio can be heard. A giggly presenter is introducing his guest—a famous character who makes a fortune in the laughter-making profession, a man whose range, says the presenter, includes affectionate and cruel humour, full-on and oblique humour, chilly, frosty and even infantile humour. He's gone to a commercial break now and the caretaker has switched off the radio.

The nights are noisy here.

My neighbour remembers his guitar, which had been silent since yesterday. Sounds of nature invade the room. That's what can be heard now—this chaos coming from the other side of the wall that is no longer a wall, but con-solidated shadows, shadow bricks you cannot knock against. And into this chaos come four rhythmic knocks. Here they come again. Four rhythmic knocks.

People we don't know are waiting for us on the shore with words of welcome mingled with smiles, words of a language we are unable to translate without that smile. And we shall have to learn how to take on the smell of these men, so that the crocodiles recognize us as their own. With rodeo-style moves and songs to keep panic at bay, they'll force the bucking waves to accept the presence of our boat, and we'll have set out on the road that will take us from the night that's ending to another one that's just beginning.

Perhaps, having got all the bitterness out of me, I shall experience that feeling Axis Kemal spoke to me about, that sense of seeking out a treasure in the darkness. And that treasure will be my own life, which was, for a time, hidden from my eyes. I've long known there's no magic formula against the roaring of storms, that there's no prayer that will calm the furious sea. There's just the intelligence of an expert at the helm, who is mas-ter, at every second, not of the wind but of his art of tack-ing, master at every second, and amazed too at each of these seconds that he was not smashed to pieces long ago. Though perfection is not of this world, I have no other word, not one, says the speaker, but perfection for each of these seconds into which no whit of vanity enters.